P9-CPV-366

"As tempting as it is to take a little detour here with you, I'm not going to."

"You're not?"

"Here's the thing," Reed declared, using her exact terminology.

It occurred to Ruby that he was not a man of almosts. He wasn't almost tall or almost handsome or almost proud. He was all those things and more. He'd drawn a line in the sand, and apparently he intended to make certain she knew exactly how far, how deep and how wide the line ran.

"The baby you saw my brother carrying before lunch?" he said. "You assumed Marsh is his father."

She stood mute, waiting for him to continue.

"Are you telling me Marsh isn't Joey's father?"

"It's possible he is." Reed's voice was deep, reverent almost, and extraordinarily serious. "But it's also possible I am."

Surely Ruby's dismay was written all over her face. But she didn't have it in her to care how she looked.

The baby she'd seen before lunch was possibly Reed's? Had she heard him correctly?

* * *

ROUND-THE-CLOCK BRIDES:
Minute by minute...hour by hour...
they'll find true love.

Dear Reader,

When I was fifteen, my brother said, "There's a guy I want you to meet." He was tall and older—sixteen. Three years later I married him, and I've loved him, and a good wedding, ever since. It's not the walk down the aisle or even what happens after that walk is over, because let's face it, a lot of hard things can happen later. What I love is the moment when two people promise to love one another forever. In that instant forever is possible; all good things are.

When I began writing my first book set in Orchard Hill, I didn't know it would launch a series called Round-the-Clock Brides. I only knew it would begin with a gift and end with a wedding. Halfway through *The Wedding Gift* I knew minor character Ruby O'Toole would star in her own book one day.

A Bride by Summer is Ruby's story. It begins with a chance encounter and ends with a promise: good things are going to happen.

Let's all believe...

Sandra

A Bride by Summer

—

Sandra Steffen

HARLEQUIN® SPECIAL EDITION®

If you purchased this book without a cover you should be aware
that this book is stolen property. It was reported as "unsold and
destroyed" to the publisher, and neither the author nor the
publisher has received any payment for this "stripped book."

Recycling programs
for this product may
not exist in your area.

ISBN-13: 978-0-373-65827-5

A BRIDE BY SUMMER

Copyright © 2014 by Sandra E. Steffen

All rights reserved. Except for use in any review, the reproduction
or utilization of this work in whole or in part in any form by any
electronic, mechanical or other means, now known or hereinafter
invented, including xerography, photocopying and recording, or in
any information storage or retrieval system, is forbidden without
the written permission of the publisher, Harlequin Enterprises Limited,
225 Duncan Mill Road, Don Mills, Ontario M3B 3K9, Canada.

This is a work of fiction. Names, characters, places and incidents are
either the product of the author's imagination or are used fictitiously, and
any resemblance to actual persons, living or dead, business establishments,
events or locales is entirely coincidental.

This edition published by arrangement with Harlequin Books S.A.

For questions and comments about the quality of this book, please contact us
at CustomerService@Harlequin.com.

® and TM are trademarks of Harlequin Enterprises Limited or its corporate
affiliates. Trademarks indicated with ® are registered in the United States Patent
and Trademark Office, the Canadian Intellectual Property Office and in other
countries.

Printed in U.S.A.

www.Harlequin.com

Books by Sandra Steffen

Harlequin Special Edition

‡*A Bride Until Midnight* #2111
‡*A Bride Before Dawn* #2153
‡*A Bride by Summer* #2345

Silhouette Special Edition

Not Before Marriage! #1061
The Wedding Gift #2050

Silhouette Romance

Child of Her Dreams #1005
*Bachelor Daddy #1028
*Bachelor at the Wedding #1045
*Expectant Bachelor #1056
Lullaby and Goodnight #1074
A Father for Always #1138
For Better, For Baby #1163
**Luke's Would-Be Bride #1230
**Wyatt's Most Wanted Wife #1241
**Clayton's Made-Over Mrs. #1253
**Nick's Long-Awaited Honeymoon #1290
The Bounty Hunter's Bride #1306
**Burke's Christmas Surprise #1337
**Wes Stryker's Wrangled Wife #1362
**McKenna's Bartered Bride #1398
**Sky's Pride and Joy #1486
**Quinn's Complete Seduction #1517
The Wolf's Surrender #1630

*Wedding Wager
**Bachelor Gulch
‡Round-the-Clock Brides

Silhouette Desire

Gift Wrapped Dad #972

Silhouette Books

36 Hours
Marriage by Contract

Fortunes of Texas
Lone Star Wedding

The Coltons
The Trophy Wife

Delivered by Christmas
  "A Christmas to Treasure"

Harlequin Next

Life Happens #10
Ex's and Oh's #29
Slightly Psychic #72

Other titles by this author
available in ebook format.

SANDRA STEFFEN

has always been a storyteller. She began nurturing this hidden talent by concocting adventures for her brothers and sisters, even though the boys were more interested in her ability to hit a baseball over the barn—an automatic home run. She didn't begin her pursuit of publication until she was a young wife and mother of four sons. Since her thrilling debut as a published author in 1992, more than thirty-five of her novels have graced bookshelves across the country.

This winner of a RITA® Award, a Wish Award and a National Readers' Choice Award enjoys traveling with her husband. Usually their destinations are settings for her upcoming books. They are empty nesters these days. Who knew it could be so much fun? Please visit her at www.sandrasteffen.com.

For my beloved brothers, Ron and Dave. Every girl should have a big brother. I was lucky enough, and so blessed, to have two.

Chapter One

Reed Sullivan wasn't an easy man to read.

Not that the two women waiting in line behind him at the drugstore in Orchard Hill weren't trying. In the security camera on the wall he saw one nudge the other before motioning to the small carton he'd pushed across the counter. The pharmacy tech held any outward display of curiosity to a discreet lift of her eyebrows as she dropped his purchase into a white paper bag.

Apparently men didn't buy paternity test kits here every day.

He didn't begrudge any of them their curiosity. Most of the time he appreciated that particular trait inherent in most women almost as much as he enjoyed the way they could change the atmosphere in a room just by entering it. He had a deep respect for women, enjoyed spending time with them, was intrigued by them and appreciated them on so many levels. He did not leave birth control to chance. And yet here he was, making a purchase he'd never imagined he would need to make.

He paid with cash, pocketed his change and left the store, by all outward appearances as cool, calm and confident as he'd been when he'd entered. Out in the parking lot, a bead of sweat trickled down his neck and under the collar of his shirt.

Reed understood profit margins and the challenges of zoning issues. Those things always made sense in the end. This was different. Nothing about this situation made sense. Gnawing worry had jolted him awake at 4:00 a.m. It didn't require great insight to understand the cause. It all centered around the innocent baby he and his brothers had discovered on their doorstep ten days ago.

The very idea that someone would abandon a baby in such a way in this day and age was ludicrous. And yet there the baby had been, unbelievably tiny and undeniably alone. Reed, Marsh and Noah were all confirmed bachelors and hadn't known the first thing about caring for a baby, but they'd picked the crying infant up and discovered a note.

Our precious son, Joseph Daniel Sullivan. I call him Joey. He's my life. I beg you take good care of him until I can return for him.

Our precious son? *Whose* precious son?

The handwritten note hadn't been addressed. Or signed.

Reed wasn't prone to self-doubt, but now he wondered if they *should* have performed a paternity test immediately. He should have insisted. What had he been thinking?

He hadn't been thinking. None of them had.

They'd spent the first week fumbling with formula and feedings, diaper changes and sleep deprivation while doing everything in their power to determine what the infant in their charge needed and wanted.

Joey had a lusty cry he wasn't afraid to use, and yet before his first night with them was over, he'd looked with burgeoning trust at the three men suddenly thrust into this new and foreign role. He didn't seem to mind their ineptitude.

Until that night, Reed and his brothers hadn't considered the possibility that one of them might have become a father without their knowledge. To make matters worse, they had no way of knowing which of the women from their respective pasts might have been desperate enough to leave Joey in such a manner. The million-dollar question remained.

Which of them was Joey's father?

Reed placed the small paper bag containing the paternity test kit on the passenger seat and started his car. As he pulled out of his parking space, the impulse to squeal his tires was strong. He quelled it because he was the middle brother, the one who thought before he reacted, who kept his wits about him and his head out of the clouds, the one with nerves of steel and the willpower to match.

Minutes later he was on Old Orchard Highway, a few miles from home. The sunroof was open, the morning breeze already fragrant and warm. The radio was off, the hum of his car's engine little balm for the uncertainties plaguing him today.

That first night, he, Marsh and Noah had put their heads together and had come up with a schedule for Joey's care, as well as a plan to try to locate his mother. It hadn't taken Noah long to find the woman from his past. A daredevil test pilot, he'd realized soon after coming face-to-face with Lacey Bell again that covert moves weren't her style. Joey wasn't Lacey's baby, and therefore Noah had been certain he wasn't his, either. That hadn't kept him from pulling out all the stops to rekindle the love affair of his life. Noah and Lacey had eloped two nights ago.

Paternity came down to Marsh or Reed.

They'd hired a private investigator to follow clues and leads regarding the whereabouts of the women who seemed to have disappeared into thin air. Under ordinary circumstances, he and Marsh didn't talk about their sex lives. If not for Joey's arrival, Reed wouldn't have known that Marsh had spent an idyllic week with a woman named Julia Monroe while on vacation last year or that she'd seemed to disappear into thin air as soon as the week was over.

Like his brothers, Reed liked to keep his private life private. There was only one woman, and one night, he couldn't account for. She was a waitress he'd met on a layover in Dallas during a business trip last year. She'd told him her name was Cookie—now he wished he'd asked a few questions. Could she have left Joey on his doorstep a year later?

He and Marsh had hired a P.I. with an impressive success rate. But so far every lead Sam Lafferty had followed had turned into a dead end. At least, once Reed and Marsh determined which of them was the baby's father, Sam could focus on finding one woman instead of two.

The test kit slid to the edge of the seat as Reed approached a banked curve in the highway. Behind him a red car that had been a speck in his rearview mirror a few seconds ago was closing in on him fast. The sports car came so close to his bumper he braced for a rear-end collision. All at once, the car swerved across the double yellow line and began to pass.

Up ahead an eighteen-wheeler was barreling around a curve straight toward them. An air horn blasted and tires screeched. The driver of the Corvette cranked the wheel to the right, thrusting his car back into Reed's lane. With no other place to go, Reed took the shoulder of the highway. He braked, but it was too late. His tires broke loose. And he started to spin.

Around and around he went, on the highway and off, from one shoulder to the other. Gravel churned and dust rose. He somehow missed an oncoming vehicle but clipped a highway sign with one of his mirrors. When he finally came to a complete stop, his engine was racing and so was his heart rate. He gripped the steering wheel, his foot pressed hard on the brake.

The dust was settling when he noticed that another car had stopped a short distance ahead of him on the opposite side of the road. The door opened. The next thing he knew, a slender, sandal-ensconced foot touched the ground.

Ruby O'Toole hit the pavement running.

She raced across the highway toward a silver Mustang sitting at an odd angle along the side of the road. The driver was looking at her through the windshield, his eyes narrowed and his jaw set. She stood back as he got out, and watched as he opened his fists and un-clenched his fingers, straightened his arms and rotated his broad shoulders, as if checking to see if everything was still operational.

"Are you okay?" she asked.

He didn't answer, making her wonder if he was in shock.

"I'm calling 911. I've seen a lot of accidents and you could have whiplash."

"I don't need an ambulance." His voice was steady and deep, but the way he put a hand on the back of his neck made her wonder if he was more shaken than he was admitting.

"It's best to err on the side of caution," she insisted. "Adrenaline and shock can mask an injury like whip-lash or a spinal column misalignment."

With a grimace, he said, "My back is fine. And I don't have whiplash." In his early thirties, he had short, sandy-blond hair and wore a gray dress shirt, the sleeves rolled partway up his forearms.

"You just never know," she argued. "The stiffness wouldn't necessarily set in until later."

He circled his car, his face impassive as he ran his hand over the Mustang's hood.

"Trust me. I'm fine."

"If you say so, but if I were you, I'd be stomping my feet and shaking my fist and swearing at that jerk who ran you off the road. You could have been killed! The creep had no right to drive like some bat out of hell. Jerks like him think they own the road and everything in their path." Catching him looking at her, she said,

"Some women cry at emergencies. I get mad. I have a temper. And don't tell me it goes with my hair."

"I won't."

She thought he might smile. When he didn't, she heard herself say, "It's what my boyfriend used to say. My ex-boyfriend. Peter. Cheater Peter." She had to clamp her mouth shut to keep from continuing. What was wrong with her?

"That explains the ex," he said in a deep, smooth voice that gave little away. As he examined his loosened mirror, he asked, "Are you an EMT?"

She'd been in the process of smoothing her hands down her shorts and straightening her tank top, and had to stop for a moment to wonder at his question. "Oh," she said. "You mean because I said I've seen a lot of accidents. No, my most recent career jag was driving a tow truck for my dad's wrecker service near Traverse City."

She didn't bother telling him that prior to working for her dad she'd spent three years with a trendsetting marketing firm in L.A. This stranger didn't need to hear how much trouble she'd had deciding what she wanted to do with her life. Reverting to small talk, she asked, "Do you live in Orchard Hill?"

"A mile from here." The breeze ruffled his blond hair and toyed with the collar of his shirt.

"I just moved here two days ago," she said. "In all likelihood, my mother is rearranging the furniture in my new apartment as I speak, while my father adds to his ever-growing list of all the reasons buying a tavern in this college town is a mistake. So, did your life pass before your eyes?"

* * *

Reed did a double take and looked at the talkative woman who'd stopped to make certain he wasn't hurt. She wore shorts that fit her to perfection and a white tank top that made her arms and shoulders appear golden. A silver charm shaped like a feather hung from a delicate chain around her neck. Her hair, long and red and curly, fluttered freely in the wind. When he found himself looking into her green eyes, he wished he'd have started there.

His gaze locked with hers, and the air went oddly still. In the ensuing silence, he wondered where the birds and the summer breeze and the traffic had gone.

Her throat convulsed slightly, as if she was having trouble breathing, too. "You're not much of a talker, are you?" she finally asked.

"Normally," he said, "I'm the one asking the questions."

She took a backward step and said, "Are you a lawyer?"

"Why, do I look like a lawyer?"

She shrugged one shoulder. "It's just that lawyers tend to ask a lot of questions."

"I'm not a lawyer."

"A journalist, then?"

"No."

"A Virgo?" she asked with a small smile.

He had to think about that one because astrology was hardly something he put stock in. "My birthday's November sixth."

"Ah, a Scorpio. You water signs are deep. And moody. Obviously." She shook herself slightly and said, "If you're sure you aren't hurt, I'll be going."

The smile she gave him went straight to places that made a man stop thinking and start imagining. It was intimate and dangerous, not to mention off-limits, given his present situation.

She glanced back at him as she opened her car door, and said, "Two-X-Z-zero-three."

"Pardon me?"

"The Corvette's license plate number." She started her car, and through the open window said, "It's two-X-Z-zero-three. I happened to notice it when the jerk flew by me at the city limit sign."

"You *happened* to notice it."

"I have a photographic memory for those kinds of details." With that, she drove away.

Reed got back behind the wheel of his car, too. When the coast was clear, he made a U-turn and continued toward home. He drove more slowly than usual, the entire episode replaying in his mind, from the uncanny near miss, to the chance encounter with the modern-day Florence Nightingale along the side of the highway. He wondered if he'd ever met anyone with a photographic memory.

The woman had asked if his life had passed before his eyes as he'd spun out of control. He hadn't seen the images of either of his brothers or his sister, or of their parents, killed so tragically years ago, or the first girl he'd kissed, or even the most recent woman. He hadn't seen his oldest friend or his newest business associate. The image in his mind as he'd spun to what might have been his death had been Joey's.

Sobered further by the realization, he pulled into his driveway and parked in his usual spot beside Marsh's

SUV. He cut the engine then felt around on the floor until he located the test kit.

For a moment, he sat there looking at the sprawling white house where he'd grown up. Beyond the 120-year-old Victorian sat the original stone cider house his great-great-grandfather had built with his own hands. Ten years ago Reed and his brothers and younger sister had converted the sprawling old barn into a bakery, where they sold donuts and baked goods, and fresh apple cider by the cup or by the gallon. There was a gift shop, too, and sheds, where their signs and equipment were stored. Behind them was the meadow where thousands of customers parked each fall. From here Reed could see the edge of the orchards, the heart and soul of the entire operation.

He hadn't planned to move back to Orchard Hill after college, but life had a way of altering plans. Reed wasn't a man who wasted a lot of time or energy wondering what he'd missed. Bringing the family business into the current century was one of his proudest achievements. His brother Marsh knew every tree on the property, every graft and every branch that needed to be pruned. Reed knew all about business plans, spreadsheets, tax laws, health inspections and zoning. He'd been the one to have visions of expansion.

Already he could picture Joey following in his footsteps one day. What was shocking was that he *wanted* Joey to follow in his footsteps. Until they'd discovered that little kid on their doorstep ten days ago, Reed hadn't realized how much he wanted to pass on the legacy of Sullivans Orchard and his business acumen to another generation.

He would be proud if Joey was his son.

With that thought front and center in his mind, he went up the sidewalk and through the unlocked screen door.

Chapter Two

Even on days when Reed swore everything was changing, there were a few things that always remained the same. Today it was the scent of strong coffee on the morning air.

He followed the unmistakable aroma into the kitchen and found his older brother at the counter across the room, pouring steaming brew into a large mug. Reed's gaze settled on Joey, nestled securely on Marsh's left arm, his eyes wide and his wispy hair sticking up in every direction.

Baby bottles filled the sink, and spilled formula pooled on the counter nearby. A load of clean baby clothes was piled in the middle of the table. It was hard to believe that two weeks ago the only items on the counter had been take-out menus, a cell phone or two and car keys.

"Did you get it?" Marsh asked without turning around.

"In the first pharmacy I tried." Reed kept his voice gentle because Joey had locked his eyes on him over Marsh's shoulder.

A toothless smile engaged Joey's entire face and brought out every fierce protective instinct Reed possessed. Everyone they'd consulted agreed that Joey appeared to be approximately three months old. The sum of the baby's age and the length of a normal pregnancy corresponded with the timing of the business trip Reed had taken to Texas last year.

"I heard from Noah," he said, sharing news from their younger brother with Marsh. Noah never had been one for long letters or phone calls, and his text was no different. Two words, hot damn, spoke volumes. "I'd say he and Lacey are pretty happy."

Joey smiled again, evidently happy, too. Already that little kid always assumed everybody was talking to him.

Reed tossed the discreet paper bag onto the table and continued toward his brother. "I'll take him. It looks as though you could use two hands for that coffee."

Joey didn't seem to mind the transition from one set of strong arms to the other. He was trusting in that way. Reed wondered if that trait came from his mother.

Paternity-wise, they weren't going to be able to make so much as an educated guess without the test, for Marsh and Reed were too closely related and nearly identical in height, bone structure and build. They were polar opposites in most other ways, however. Dark where Reed was fair, brown-eyed to Reed's blue-gray, whisker stubble where Reed was clean-shaven, Marsh was two and a half years older. Today he wore his usual faded jeans, scuffed work boots and a holey T-shirt Reed hadn't seen in years.

It reminded Reed that practically every item of clothing they owned was dirty. They needed help around here with laundry and dishes and especially with Joey's care, which was why they were interviewing someone later this morning. Luckily, Joey seemed oblivious to the havoc his arrival had brought. Tipping the scales at eleven and a half pounds, he was a handsome, sturdy baby with hair as dark as Marsh's and eyes that were gray-blue like Reed's.

"Hi, buddy," Reed said with more emotion than he'd known he was capable of feeling for a child so small. He carried the baby to the table and took a seat. "Is this formula still good?" he asked his brother.

Marsh looked at his watch, nodded, and Reed offered the baby the last ounce in the bottle. As Joey drank, he looked up at him and wrapped his entire hand around Reed's little finger. Reed was growing accustomed to the way his heart swelled, crowding his chest.

He'd read a tome's worth of information and suggestions about how to care for infants these past ten days. Maybe the way Joey grasped the finger of whoever was feeding him was reflexive. Reed was of the opinion that it had more to do with being a Sullivan, which among other things meant he wanted what he wanted when he wanted it.

Marsh was leaning against the counter across the room, ankles crossed as he somberly sipped his coffee. "How many times do you think we waited out the night sitting around that table?"

"During Noah's rebellious years—which was most

of them—and last year with Madeline? Too many to count," Reed said.

It reminded them both that they weren't novices when it came to handling tough situations. After their parents were killed in an icy pileup on the interstate thirteen years ago, twenty-three-year-old Marsh had suddenly become the head of the family. Reed had nearly doubled his class load at Purdue, and as soon as he graduated a year later, he'd come home to help. Noah had been a hell-raising seventeen-year-old then. Their sister, Madeline, had been fourteen and was struggling to adjust to a world that had changed overnight. It was hard to believe Noah and Madeline were both married now.

"This feels different, doesn't it?" Reed said, looking into Joey's sleepy little face.

"Different in every way," Marsh agreed.

Marsh tore the paternity test kit package open, read the directions and then handed them to Reed, who carefully moved Joey to the crook of his left arm, then read them, too. They filled out the forms with their pertinent information and followed the instructions to the letter before sealing everything in the accompanying airtight sleeves.

"What do you think Dad would say if he were here?" Reed asked as he closed the mailing carton.

"After the shock wore off, he probably wouldn't say much," Marsh answered quietly. "Mom would be the one we'd have to worry about."

Reed and Marsh shared a smile that took them back to when they were teenagers. Reed said, "She'd expect us to do the right thing. They both would."

"We are doing the right thing, or at least as close

to the right thing as we can under the circumstances," Marsh said. "Have you decided what you're going to do if Joey is yours?"

Reed eyed the baby now sleeping in his arms. If Joey was his son, it meant Joey's mother was the curvy blonde waitress named Cookie who'd accidentally spilled chili in his lap during a layover in Dallas last year. She'd blushed and apologized and somehow, when her shift was over, they'd wound up back at her place.

"If it turns out Joey's mine, and Sam locates Cookie and she has a legitimate reason for leaving him, I'd like to get to know her better." He wished he'd asked more questions that night. She'd mentioned an ex-husband, somewhere, and a local play she'd been auditioning for. He didn't recall ever hearing her last name. Now he wished he had asked. After all, if she was the mother of his son, she deserved better. She deserved the chance to explain. "What about you? What will you do if the test proves Joey is yours?"

Marsh took his time considering his reply. "The week I spent with Julia on the Outer Banks last year was pretty damn idyllic. I thought I knew her as well as a man could know a woman. I thought we had something. If Joey is our son, she would have had to have a very good reason for all of this. The Julia I knew wouldn't have left Joey unless she had no other choice. I have a hundred questions, but it does no good to imagine what might have happened to her or what might be happening to her now. I only know that if Julia is Joey's mother and I am his father, she will return for him, and when that happens I'd like to try to work things out, as a family."

It wasn't surprising that they wanted the same thing, for Reed and Marsh were both family men at heart. They grew silent, each lost in his own thoughts. The only sound in the room was Joey's hum as he slept in Reed's arms and the tick of the clock on the old stove.

"Why don't you put Joey in his crib for his morning nap," Marsh suggested. "The agency is sending another woman out for an interview later. You should have plenty of time to overnight the paternity kit and be back before then. Unless you want me to mail it."

"You had the late shift with Joey," Reed said. "I'll take the kit to the post office."

After laying Joey in his crib in the home office they'd converted into a nursery last week, he returned to the kitchen, where Marsh was still somberly sipping coffee. Keys in one hand and the sealed test kit in the other, Reed headed for the door.

"Hey, Reed?" Marsh stood across the room, his jeans riding low, his stance wide, his brown eyes hooded. "May the best man win."

Again, that grin took Reed back to when they were kids and everything was a competition. He shook his head, but he couldn't help grinning a little, too.

Getting in his car with its loosened side mirror, he wondered if Marsh was picturing Julia right now. Reed could only wonder what might have prompted Joey's mother—whoever she was—to leave him with only a vague note and a loose promise to return for him.

He was at the end of the driveway when it occurred to him that he couldn't seem to bring Cookie into sharp focus in his memory. Her bleached-blond hair kept switching to red.

* * *

"How was your drive?" Ruby's closest friend, Amanda Moore, asked the minute Ruby got back. "Tell me you got completely lost."

Ruby shook her head. "Sorry to disappoint you, but no."

"Not even slightly turned around?" Because Amanda had been lost when she'd met her fiancé, Todd, she was convinced that the key to finding happiness was that sensation she'd experienced when she'd made a wrong turn but somehow wound up in the right place.

But as Ruby had told her a hundred times, she didn't get lost. Ever. Her innate sense of direction was intricately linked to her keen memory for all things visual. Both had gotten her out of countless scrapes over the years.

"The reunion is in just over two weeks." Amanda was tapping away on her notebook at the end of the bar in Ruby's new tavern. "That doesn't leave us very much time to find you a date."

"You're my best friend, and I would give you a kidney or the shirt off my back," Ruby declared from behind the bar. "But I told you. I'm not taking a date. From now on I'm flying solo. I mean it, Amanda." Her laptop was open, too. Next to it was the box she'd started filling with cameras from the former owner's collection. "I don't even *want* to attend the class reunion."

"You have to, Ruby."

"Peter's going to be there."

"I know," Amanda said gently. "That's why I think you should bring a date. As former class officers, we're not only the planning committee, but we're the welcoming committee, too. Don't even think about trying to get out of it. You promised, and you never break your promises."

With a sigh, Ruby returned to compiling the menu of drinks that would be indigenous to her saloon. So far her list included alcoholic beverages with names such as Howl at the Moon and Fountain of Youth and Dynamite. Since she thought best when she was moving, she wandered to the pool tables in the back of the room.

Amanda tucked her chin-length brown hair behind one ear and followed. "Number one," she said, fine-tuning a line on the small screen. "This goes without saying because it's always number one with you. Nonetheless, number one." She cleared her throat for emphasis. "He must be tall. T-a-l-l. Tall, with a capital *T.* Number two. It would be nice if he spoke in complete sentences."

Ruby rolled her eyes. While she was looking up at the ceiling, a loud scrape sounded from above. Evidently her mother was still rearranging her furniture, even though Ruby had told her that the layout was fine the way it was.

Nobody listened to her, she thought as she shook out the plush sleeping bag she'd found near the pool tables and refolded it. It was a strange place to leave a sleeping bag, but at the closing yesterday, the previous owner, Lacey Bell Sullivan, had asked Ruby to keep the bedroll here for safekeeping for a few days while Lacey's brand-new husband whisked her away on their honeymoon. Lacey had vaguely mentioned that someone might come by to pick it up. Ruby believed there was something Lacey wasn't telling her, but Amanda was right. To Ruby, a promise was a promise.

Amanda was rattling off number five, apparently unconcerned that Ruby had missed numbers three and four entirely. "No bodybuilding Mr. America wannabes. And your date should be sensitive but not too sensitive. You don't want to be apologizing all the time."

Ruby smiled in spite of herself.

While Amanda recited the remaining must-have qualities from her list, Ruby took another look around. It was hard to believe this building was hers. The main room of the saloon was large and L-shaped, stretching from Division Street all the way to the alley out back. The tables and chairs were mismatched and the lighting questionable. There was a jukebox on one wall and two pool tables in need of a little restoration in the back. The ornately carved bar, where drinks would be served and stories swapped, was the crowning jewel of the entire room.

The ceilings were low and two of the walls were exposed brick. The hardwood floors were worn and the restrooms needed a little updating, but the building was structurally sound and included an apartment with a separate entrance.

Lacey Bell Sullivan had moved to Orchard Hill with her father when she was twelve. She'd inherited the building when he died. Business had fallen off, but she believed with all her heart that what the tavern really needed was a breath of fresh air. A new life.

Ruby thrilled at the thought.

"Rainbow of Optimism," she said under her breath as she hurried back to her laptop and added another drink title to her menu.

Amanda hopped back onto her barstool, the pert

bounce of her hairstyle matching her personality. "What are you working on?"

"I'm giving Bell's a new identity so it will appeal to a lively, energetic, fun-loving crowd. Right now I'm compiling a menu featuring one-of-a-kind drinks."

Amanda turned the screen around in order to read the menu. "These are fun, Ruby. Fountain of Youth and Dynamite are self-explanatory. What's this two-X-Z-zero-three?"

"Oh, that doesn't belong on the list. It's just the license plate number of a Corvette I saw run a sweet Mustang off the road earlier. I stopped to make sure the driver of the Mustang was okay. What do you think of Happy Hops?"

"Was this driver a guy?"

"We're talking about the title of a drink," Ruby insisted. "Is Happy Hops too trite?"

"Was this handsome stranger under, say, thirty-five?" Amanda asked.

"I didn't say he was handsome."

"I knew it," Amanda quipped.

Another scrape sounded overhead. Holding up one hand, Ruby said, "You and my parents are making me sincerely wish I had hired a moving company."

Just then Ruby's father came bounding into the room waving a sheet of yellow lined paper. A brute of a man with a shock of red hair and a booming voice, he said, "The smoke alarm doesn't work. The bathroom faucet drips. Only one burner works on the stove, and that refrigerator is as old as I am. Did you count the steps leading to the apartment? Do you really want to have to climb twenty steps at the end of a long day?"

"Walter, would you stop?" The only person who

called Red O'Toole Walter was his wife. Ruby's mother now joined them downstairs. The freckles scattered across Scarlet O'Toole's nose gave her a perpetually young appearance, which was at odds with the streaks of gray in her short red hair.

"It isn't too late for her to get out of this," Red said to his wife.

Scarlet wasn't paying attention. She was listening to Amanda, who was telling her about the near accident Ruby had witnessed and the driver she'd stopped to help earlier.

"Was he tall?" Scarlet quizzed her daughter's best friend.

"I asked her that, too," Amanda replied. "That particular detail has not been forthcoming. Yet."

Ruby dropped her face into her hands.

"She needs to come home with us," her father insisted, as if that was that.

"She signed the papers," her mother said dismissively.

"I don't like the idea of our little girl serving up hard liquor to a bunch of rowdy m-e-n."

Ruby didn't bother reminding them that she was standing right here.

"Driving a tow truck you were okay with." Ruby's mother had a way of wrinkling up her nose when she was making a rhetorical statement. She demonstrated the tactic, and then said, "She's only a three-and-a-half-hour drive away."

Ruby backed away from the trio—not that any of them noticed—and traipsed to her laptop, where she added another one-of-a-kind drink title to the top of her menu. Kerfuffle. If her life thus far was any indication, this one was going to be a big seller.

"It's time for you to go," she said loudly enough to be heard over the din.

All three turned to face her.

"What?" her mother asked.

"But I'm not finished—" her father grumbled.

"You're kicking us out?" Amanda groused.

Ruby stood her ground. "Thanks for all your help these past two days. I mean that from the bottom of my heart."

"You're asking us to leave?" her six-foot-three-inch father asked incredulously.

"I'm begging you," she said.

"See what you've done?" Scarlet said to Red.

"So I'm worried that my little girl is a barkeeper."

Red O'Toole's little girl was twenty-eight years old and stood almost five foot eleven. But she smiled at him as she rounded the bar to give him a daughterly kiss on the cheek and a heartfelt hug. "The smoke alarm probably just needs a new battery. One burner and a microwave is all I need. I can deal with the leaky faucet, and those steps will be a good workout."

Heaving a sigh that seemed to originate from the vicinity of his knees, her father said, "Isn't there some legal provision that allows you three days to change your mind?"

"Even if there was a provision like that, I wouldn't back out of this," she said gently but firmly. "I like this town and I especially like this bar. I feel a connection to this place. I can't explain it, but I want to make it a success. It's going to be a challenge, but I can do this. I know I can."

"Don't worry, dear, you still have me," Scarlet said to Red. "And Rusty. If you want to worry about one of your children, worry about him. Our daughter's right. We should be getting back to Gale. She's going to have plenty to do putting her furniture back the way she had it. Isn't that right, honey?"

Ruby pulled a face, for her mother knew her well.

"Are you coming, Amanda?" Scarlet asked.

"I rode with Ruby, remember?" Amanda said. "I either have to catch a ride home with you two or take a bus. But nobody's going anywhere until she answers my question." She spun around again and faced Ruby. "Details would be good."

"Details about what?" Ruby's innocent expression didn't fool anybody.

"What was the guy driving that sweet Mustang like?" Amanda asked, sounding like the kindergarten teacher she was.

Even Ruby's father waited for Ruby's reply.

"What was he like?" Ruby echoed, seriously considering the question. "Let's see. He didn't slam his car door or kick the no-passing sign even though it took out one of his mirrors."

She saw the looks passing between her mother and her best friend. There was nothing she could do about what they were thinking.

"Patient isn't on my list," Amanda said, "but it should be. What else?"

With a sigh of surrender, Ruby said, "He was blond and well dressed and understandably irritated but polite."

"And?" Amanda stood up straight, as if doing so would make her less dwarfed by the three tall redheads.

"And that's all," Ruby stated.

"That's all?" Amanda echoed.

"Isn't that what she said?" her father asked gruffly.

"But, honey," Ruby's mother implored.

"Was he tall?" Amanda and Scarlet asked in unison.

Ruby opened her mouth, closed it, skewed her mouth to one side and finally shrugged. "I didn't notice."

"You didn't notice?" her mother asked gently.

"But height is *always* what you notice first," Amanda insisted.

"I told you. I'm not interested in finding a man. Maybe I'll get a dog. Perhaps a rescue with a heart-breaking past and soulful eyes."

"You're bound to run into him again, you know," Scarlet said, and very nearly smiled.

"Since you didn't hear me, I'll say it again. I'm finished with men. All men. For good."

There were hugs all around and a few tears, but those were mostly from her father. Ruby promised her mother she would call. She promised her father she would keep her doors locked. When Amanda reminded her that the reunion was in two weeks' time, Ruby reluctantly reconfirmed her promise that she would be there, too.

Finally, she stood in the hot sun in the back alley, waving as her parents and best friend drove away. Alone at last, she returned to the tavern and looked around the dimly lighted room. She had a lot to do, from remodeling to advertising to hiring waitstaff. Already she could see the new Bell's in her imagination. There would be soft lighting and lively music and laminated menus featuring one-of-a-kind drinks and people talking and laughing and maybe even falling in love. Not her, of course. But friends would gather here, and some of them would become her friends, and all of them would be part of her new life.

Happiness bubbled out of her. No matter what her father claimed, buying a boarded-up tavern in Orchard Hill wasn't a mistake.

She happened to catch her reflection in the beveled mirror behind the bar. Chestnut-red wouldn't have been her first choice in hair color and she'd never particularly liked her natural curls. Her face was too narrow and her lips too full, in her opinion, but her eyes were wide and green, and for the first time in a long time, there was a spark of excitement in them.

She hadn't made a mistake, not this time. Buying this tavern on a whim was the first thing she'd done in too long that was brave and a little wild, like the girl she used to be. She hugged herself, thinking how much she'd missed that.

Once again, the near accident she'd witnessed replayed through her mind.

Had the driver of the Mustang been tall?

Normally she had only to blink to bring the particulars into focus. In this instance her snapshot memory didn't include that detail.

Thinking about her history and her recent decision regarding singlehood, she decided to take that as a good sign, and left it at that.

Chapter Three

Two hours after her parents and Amanda left, Ruby stood tapping her foot on the sidewalk at the corner of Jefferson and Division Streets. She wasn't thinking about the quote she'd requested from the electrician or the baffling little mystery regarding the sleeping bag folded neatly on one of the pool tables in her tavern. She wasn't even thinking about the broodingly attractive man she'd encountered on Orchard Highway earlier. Well, she wasn't thinking about him very much.

She was thinking that if the walk sign didn't light soon, she was going to take her chances with the oncoming traffic, because she was starving.

At long last, the light changed and the window-shoppers ahead of her started across, Ruby close behind them. There was a spring in her step as she completed the last little jaunt to the restaurant at the top of the hill.

Inside, it was standing room only. People huddled together in small groups while they waited for a table.

Ruby made her way toward a handwritten chalk menu on the adjacent wall and began pondering her options. The door opened and closed several times as more people crowded into the foyer. Ruby was contemplating the lunch specials when someone jostled her from behind.

"Sorry about that," a tall man with a very small baby said, visibly trying to give her a little room.

Ruby rarely got caught staring, but there was something oddly familiar about the man. He had dark hair and an angular jaw and brown eyes. Upon closer inspection, she was certain she'd never seen him before.

He eased sideways to make room for someone trying to leave, and Ruby found herself smiling at the baby.

With a wave of his little arms, the little boy smiled back at her. "He likes you," the father said.

"It's this hair." She twirled a long lock and watched the baby's smile grow.

"You aren't by any chance looking for a job, are you?" the man asked.

Voices rose and silverware clattered and someone's cell phone rang. Through the din she wondered if she'd heard correctly.

"Provided you have never been arrested, don't lie, steal, cheat on your taxes or have a library book overdue, that is," he added.

She took a step back. "Um, that is, I mean—"

"Forgive me." Unlike the baby, this man didn't appear to be someone who smiled easily. In his mid-thirties, he looked tired and earnest and completely sincere. "It's just that Joey didn't take one look at you and start screaming."

She took a deep breath of warm, fragrant air and noticed that someone else was entering through the heavy front door. The crowd parted, making room for the newcomer. Suddenly she was standing face-to-face with the man she'd encountered along Old Orchard Highway earlier.

He looked surprised, too, but he recovered quickly and said, "Hello, again." He gave her one of those swift, thorough glances men have perfected over the ages. His eyes looked gray in this light, his face lean and chiseled. "I see you've met my brother Marsh."

Did he say brother?

She glanced from one to the other. But of course. No wonder the man holding the baby looked familiar. These two were brothers.

"I'm Reed Sullivan, by the way."

Upon hearing the name Sullivan, she said, "Ruby O'Toole. Do you by any chance know Lacey Bell Sullivan?"

"We've known Lacey forever," Marsh said. "Two days ago she married our younger brother, Noah."

"How do you know our new sister-in-law?" This time it was Reed who spoke.

And she found her gaze locked with his. "I bought Bell's Tavern from Lacey. I'm a little surprised to run into you again so soon," she said. "I mean, one chance encounter is one thing."

"Is that what this is?" Reed asked. "A chance encounter?"

His hair was five shades of blond in this light, his

skin tan. There were lines beside his eyes, and something intriguing in them.

Something came over her, settling deeper, slowly tugging at her insides. She couldn't think of anything to say, and that was unusual for her. Reed's gaze remained steady on hers, and it occurred to her that he wasn't talking anymore, either.

He was looking at her with eyes that saw God only knew what. It made these chance encounters feel heaven-sent, and that made her heart speed up and her thoughts warm.

In some far corner of her mind, she knew she had to say something, do something. She could have mentioned that she'd met their sister, Madeline, a few months ago, but that made this feel even more like destiny, and that simply wouldn't do. Someone mentioned the weather, and she was pretty sure Reed said something about the Tigers.

Normally, the weather and baseball were safe topics. They would have been safe today, but Reed smiled, and Ruby lost all sensation in her toes. Moments ago, the noise in the room had been almost deafening. Suddenly, voices faded and the clatter of silverware ceased.

Ruby's breath caught just below the little hollow at the base of her throat and a sound only she could hear echoed deep inside her chest. Part sigh, part low croon, it slowly swept across her senses.

In some far corner of her mind, she was aware that Marsh said something. He spoke again. After the third time, Reed looked dazedly at his brother.

"Our table's ready," Marsh explained.

It took Ruby a moment to gather her wits, but she

finally found her voice. "It was nice meeting you," she said to Marsh.

Her gaze locked with Reed's again. She wasn't sure what had just happened between them, but something had. She'd heard about moments like this; she'd even read about them, but she'd never experienced one quite like it herself. Until today.

After giving him a brief nod, she wended her way through the crowded room toward the counter to order her lunch to go. Initially she'd planned to wait for a table. Instead, she fixed her eyes straight ahead while her take-out order was being filled. All the while, her heart seemed intent upon fluttering up into her throat.

It was a relief when she walked out into the bright sunshine, the white paper bag that contained her lunch in her hand, her oversize purse hanging from her shoulder. Dazedly donning a pair of sunglasses, she hurried down the sidewalk. She'd reached the corner before the haze began to clear in her mind. Up ahead, two young girls were having their picture taken in front of the fountain on the courthouse square and several veterans were gathered around the flagpole.

Ruby skidded to a stop and looked around. *Where was she?*

She glanced to the right and to the left, behind her at the distance she'd come, then ahead where the sun glinted off the bronze sculpture on the courthouse lawn. With rising dismay, she shook her head.

She was going the wrong way.

"Care to tell me what you're doing?" Marsh asked Reed after the waitress cleared their places.

Decorated in classic Americana diner style, the Hill

had its original black-and-white tile floors, booths with chrome legs and benches covered in red vinyl. Other than the menu, which had been adapted to modern tastes and trends, very little had changed. The Sullivans had been coming here for years. This was the first time they'd brought a baby with them, however.

Reed double-checked the buckles on Joey's car seat. The baby's head was up, his feet were down and the straps weren't twisted. Ten days ago he hadn't known the correct way to fasten an infant safely into a car seat. That first week had been one helluva crash course for all three of them, but now Reed could buckle Joey into this contraption with his eyes closed. He could prepare a bottle when he was half asleep, too. Even diaper changing was getting easier.

Sliding to the end of his side of the booth, he said, "I'm buckling Joey into this car seat. What does it look like I'm doing?"

"You noticed nothing unusual here today?" Marsh countered in a quiet voice strong enough to penetrate steel.

"If you have a point, make it. I don't have time to play Twenty Questions," Reed declared.

"You don't seem concerned that the judge joined us for lunch," Marsh said, digging into his pocket for the tip.

Ivan Sullivan was one of those men few people liked but most couldn't help respecting.

After discovering Joey on their doorstep ten days ago, Marsh, Reed and Noah had paid their great-uncle a visit at the courthouse. An abandoned minor child was no laughing matter, and no one had been laughing as the brothers fell into rank in the judge's chambers. The note clearly stated that Joey was a Sullivan, and they'd had every intention of caring for him themselves while they unraveled this puzzle. In order for Joey to remain under their care, they were to keep the judge apprised of Joey's progress in detailed, weekly in-person reports.

Reed glanced over the heads of other diners and watched his great-uncle cut a path to the door. The way the aging judge tapped his cane on the floor with his every step only added to his haughtiness. Today's interrogation had been impromptu, but it was completely in keeping with his character. Surely, Marsh agreed.

His older brother left the tip on the table and Reed picked up the car seat with Joey strapped securely inside. Showing up in public with the baby had been the private investigator's suggestion. Arguably the most successful P.I. in the state, Sam Lafferty was banking on the possibility that seeing Marsh and Reed with Joey would stir up a little gossip and perhaps jar someone's memory of having seen an unknown woman with a small baby in the area.

"We're doing our best to care for Joey," Reed insisted. "The judge knows that. We leveled with him today."

"We?" Marsh countered. "He asked what steps we're taking to locate Joey's mother and why we haven't hired a permanent nanny and how much Joey weighs and where he sleeps. You, who can outtalk most politicians, barely said boo."

"I wouldn't go that far," Reed argued.

"That a fact?"

Reed narrowed his eyes at his brother's tone. And waited.

"You ordered the salmon," Marsh said offhandedly.

"That was salmon?" Reed asked.

Marsh slanted him a look not unlike the judge's. "You had meat loaf. It arrived with a loaded baked potato just the way I ordered it. Shelly mixed up our plates. You dug into my lunch the moment she set it in front of you."

With his sinking feeling growing stronger, Reed raked his fingers through his hair, for surely the shrewdest judge in the county had noticed Reed's faux pas. If he and Marsh were going to keep Joey out of the system, neither of them had better display so much as a hint of poor behavior.

They walked outside together and stood shoulder to shoulder beneath the red-and-white awning shading the restaurant's facade.

Grasping the handle of the car seat firmly in his right hand, Reed let the seat dangle close to the ground, simulating a rocking motion that was lulling Joey to sleep. "I owe you," he said. "You don't even like salmon."

"It's nothing you wouldn't have done for me, but that was some reaction you had to the redhead who bought Lacey's place."

A city crew was working on a burst water main at the bottom of the hill on Division Street, and traffic was being rerouted. Unbidden, Reed's thoughts took a little detour, too, over long legs and creamy skin and amazing hair and green eyes that had locked with his.

"Holy hell," he muttered under his breath.

He didn't get any argument from Marsh.

A horn honked at a delivery truck parked in the left-turn lane and three boys with shaggy hair and black

T-shirts raced by on skateboards. A meter reader was marking tires and three old men were talking in front of the post office. It was just another ordinary summer day in Orchard Hill, and yet nothing had felt ordinary to Reed and Marsh in the past ten days. Joey's arrival had changed their lives, and neither of them could shake the feeling that something monumental was coming.

Their phones rang moments apart, startling them both.

Reed fished his phone out of his pocket, and over the booming bass of a passing car's radio, he said, "Yes, Sam, I'm here. Slow down."

When it came to investigative work, Sam Lafferty didn't mince words. Reed listened carefully to the latest report while keeping his end of the conversation to simple yes-and-no answers.

Marsh's call ended first. After a few minutes, Reed slipped his phone back into his pocket, too. Waiting until two dog walkers were out of hearing range, he said, "Sam located another woman named Julia Monroe."

He had Marsh's undivided attention.

"According to Sam, she's five feet tall, has curly blond hair, a doting husband and a six-month-old baby daughter who looks just like her."

Joey's eyelashes fluttered as he slept. Reed wondered if he was dreaming of his mother. He didn't know if that was possible, but lately a great deal had happened that he'd never imagined was possible.

"The Julia I know is five-six and has dark hair."

Marsh's voice sounded strained and his disappointment over yet another dead end was almost palpable. He wanted a resolution to this as much as Reed did.

"Sam is following every lead he has on both Cookie and Julia," Reed said. "He'll locate Joey's mother. Or she'll return for him, as she said in her note. We need to be prepared either way, to do what's best for Joey *either way,* and we're working on that. We are. You know it and I know it. Who was your call from?"

"It was Lacey," Marsh answered. "She and Noah stopped in Vegas and decided to spend the rest of their honeymoon there. She wants one of us to pick up those old cameras her dad used to display on the shelves behind the bar at Bell's."

"Why don't you take Joey home," Reed said. "I'll get the cameras and be right behind you."

"Are you sure that's a good idea?"

Obviously Marsh was thinking of Reed's reaction to Bell's new owner. But Reed was determined to stay levelheaded as he awaited the eventual outcome of the paternity test they'd performed that very morning. If the results of that test indicated that Joey was Reed's son, Reed's life would include Joey's mother in one capacity or another. Until they knew for sure, he had no intention of getting involved with anyone.

"Maybe I should collect those cameras," Marsh said.

"I'll go," Reed said. "Don't worry, I have this under control."

The last time Reed had been summoned to the alley behind Bell's Tavern, he'd had every intention of calmly talking Noah out of a fight. He'd wound up with a sore fist and a bruised jaw. When it was over, he and Noah had brushed the alley dust off their shoes and walked away, leaving the three troublemakers sitting in the dirt.

The alley was paved now, the steps leading to the second-story apartment freshly painted. Determined to maintain a far greater degree of restraint this afternoon, he parked beside Ruby O'Toole's sky-blue Chevy. He would knock on her door, politely ask for Lacey's cameras and then leave. If he felt so much as a stirring of red-hot anything, he would douse it before it spread.

Cool, calm and collected, he started up the stairs. At the top, he knocked briskly. In a matter of seconds the lock scraped and the door was thrown open, and Ruby O'Toole was squinting against the bright sunlight, hard-rock music blasting behind her.

"Isn't that Metallica?" he asked.

"Are you taking a survey?"

Reed had the strongest inclination to laugh out loud, and it was the last thing he'd expected. Ruby wasn't laughing, however, so he curbed his good humor, as well.

She'd put her hair up since lunch. Several curls had already pulled free. The hem of her white tank had crept up at her waist and a strap had slipped off one shoulder, revealing a faint trail of freckles that drew his gaze. The ridges of her collarbones looked delicate, her skin golden. He couldn't help noticing the little hollow at the base of her neck, where a vein was pulsing.

"I'm in the middle of something here," she said huffily as a curl fluttered freely to the side of her neck. "So, if you don't mind—"

Subtle she wasn't.

"You're busy," he said. "I'll come back at a better time."

She was shaking her head before he'd uttered the last word. "Oh no you don't. Uh-uh." Gritting her teeth, she said, "That isn't what I meant."

Two motorcycles chugged into the alley, the riders conversing over their revving engines. Stifling irritation that seemed to be directed toward him, she opened the door a little farther and said, "You might as well come in."

She didn't add *Enter at your own risk,* but she might as well have. Again, he had the strongest inclination to smile. His curiosity piqued, he followed her inside.

He closed the door but remained near it as he looked around. The living room had dark paneled walls and high ceilings and worn oak floors. A doorway on the left led to the kitchen. On the right was a shadowy hallway.

Ruby veered around half of a large sectional sitting at an odd angle in the center of the room and didn't stop until she reached a low table on the far wall. Her back to him, she quickly reached down for the volume button on an old stereo. No seeing man could have kept his eyes off the seat of those tight little shorts.

She spun around and caught him looking. While she narrowed her eyes, he reminded himself he had a legitimate reason for being here.

He'd come to—

It had to do with—

Discretion. Yes, that was it. And valor, and honor and responsibility and, huh, other important things, he was sure.

Apparently experiencing a little technical difficulty with the neurons in his brain, he took a moment to reacclimatize. It wasn't easy, but he forced his gaze away and once again looked around the room. An old trunk had been pushed against the wall, a carpet rolled up in front of it. There was an overstuffed chair and a floor lamp, too, and a few dozen boxes stacked two and three high. The fact that she'd been unpacking and arranging heavy furniture explained the sheen of perspiration on her face. He wasn't sure what to make of her irritation.

"Is something wrong, Ruby?" he asked.

Wrong? What could possibly be wrong?

Ruby didn't know whether to huff or, gosh darn it, swoon. She'd never really cared for her name, and yet Reed Sullivan made it sound like a treasure. He had one of those clear, deep voices perfectly suited for late-night radio shows and the dark. She almost wished he would keep talking.

He couldn't seem to keep his eyes off her. Unfortunately, she couldn't keep hers off him, either.

He wore dark pants and a dove-gray shirt, and it must have been hours since he'd shaved. He'd politely kept his distance, and yet the shadow of beard stubble on his jaw suggested a vein of the uncivilized. Her imagination took a little stroll that made the possibilities seem endless. The fact was, she liked the way he looked in that shirt and she was fairly certain she would like the way he looked with the buttons undone, too.

Whoa. She had to put a stop to this.

She'd made a promise to herself. She'd listed her goals when Amanda and her parents had been here hours ago. They had to do with pride and determination and succeeding and nothing to do with the way the air heated and her senses heightened every time she came within ten feet of Reed Sullivan.

She gave herself a firm mental shake and reminded herself that she really needed to focus. "Here's the thing," she said sternly.

There was a slight narrowing of his eyes, but he remained near the door, watching her, waiting for her to continue. His brows were straight and slightly darker than his hair, his face all angles and planes, his lips parted just enough to reveal the even edges of his teeth. She wondered what his mouth would feel like against her lips, her throat, her—

Grinding her molars together, she straightened her spine. She supposed she couldn't legitimately fault him for the color of his eyes or the way his pants rode low at his waist.

She blinked and refocused.

While the fan whirred behind her, she said, "I've been known to make bad choices, but I've never gotten thoroughly lost and I'm not about to start now. Do you understand?"

"This has something to do with getting lost?" he asked.

"I went the wrong way today, but I was not lost."

"I see."

He was being polite again, and patient, which only increased her frustration. Holding out her hand in a halting gesture, she said, "Yes, you're tall, with a capital *T.* And you have a slightly sinful smile you don't overuse. All that aside, you're just another good-looking guy in a fine broadcloth shirt. No offense."

"None taken." There went that sinful smile he didn't overuse. And there went the feeling in her toes.

She sighed. "It's true that I have fly-by-the-seat-of-my-pants tendencies. My father expects my new business venture to fail, and my cheating ex-boyfriend believes I'll come crawling back, and maybe I have made rash decisions in the past, but I never get lost. It has to do with my photographic memory. Technically it's called eidetic imagery."

He assumed a thoughtful pose, his left arm folded across his ribs, his chin resting on his fist.

Ruby's clothes were beginning to feel constricting, her bottom lip the slightest bit pouty and her pulse fluttery. And her toes, well, blast her toes.

While twenty-year-old heavy-metal music played in the background far more softly than Aerosmith ever intended, Reed rested his hands confidently on his hips and said, "In essence, you're saying you got lost today and it had something to do with me."

"Not lost," she countered. "Slightly turned around. I don't want— I just don't think— I shouldn't." She shook her head, straightened her spine. "I won't."

The old stereo shut off. Without music, the whir of the fan was a lonesome hum in the too-warm room.

"I'm spontaneous," she said, trying to explain. "Unfortunately, I bore easily. Believe me, it's a curse. I had a dream job in L.A. that I hated, and now I'm here, and I don't want to go back to my dad's towing service. I bought this tavern and I need to focus on getting it open and running and keeping it that way, not on some guy who, it turns out, is *tall*."

"With a capital *T*." He met her steadfast gaze. "Isn't that how you put it?"

The air heated and her thoughts slowed. It was all she could do not to smile.

Time passed slowly. Or perhaps it stopped altogether. She found herself staring into his blue-gray eyes, and doing so changed everything, until there was only this moment in time.

She swallowed. Breathed.

Yes, he was tall, she thought, and he didn't scream expletives after he'd been run off the road, and the color of his eyes was as dense and changeable as storm clouds. It was unfortunate that staring into them had wiped out the feeling in her toes, but it wasn't his fault.

"Ruby?" Reed said.

"Yes?"

"I stopped by to pick up Lacey's cameras."

She blinked. For a second there she thought he said he'd stopped by to pick up Lacey's cameras.

Ohmygod. That's what he said.

She hadn't blushed since she was thirteen years old and she really hoped she didn't start again now. Since the floor failed to open up and swallow her whole, she whirled around, stuck her stupid tingly toes into the nearest pair of flip-flops, grabbed the key ring off the peg in the kitchen and started for the door.

She darted past him, down the stairs and around the barrel of purple-and-yellow petunias blooming at the bottom. Every concise little thud the heels of his Italian loafers made on the stairs let her know he was following her.

She unlocked the tavern's back door, and as the heavy steel monstrosity swung in on creaking hinges, she said, "You could have stopped me."

Surprisingly, his voice came from little more than two feet behind her. "Only a fool would stop a beautiful woman when she's insinuating she's profoundly attracted to him, too."

Ruby must have turned around, because she and

Reed stood face-to-face, nearly toe to toe, his head tilted down slightly, hers tilted up. Holding her breath, she found herself wondering why it seemed that the smallest words in the English language were always the most poignant and powerful.

Too, Reed had said.

She was profoundly attracted to him, *too.*

That meant he was profoundly attracted to her, *also.*

They were profoundly attracted to each other.

Lord help her, she was reacting to this profound attraction again, to his nearness and the implications and nearly every wild and wonderful possibility that came with it. His gaze roamed over her entire face as if he liked what he saw. As the clock on the courthouse chimed the quarter hour and a horn honked in the distance, Ruby's heart fluttered into her throat, her toes tingling crazily and her thoughts spinning like moons around a newly discovered planet.

She and Reed seemed to realize in unison how close they were and how easy it would be to lean in those last few inches until their lips touched. If that happened, it would undoubtedly be incredible and there was no telling where it would lead. Fine. There was a very good chance it would lead to sex, wild, fast, ready, middle-of-the-day sex that spiraled into a crescendo of adrenaline and exploding electricity not unlike the music she'd been listening to before she was so rudely—okay, not that rudely—interrupted.

They stilled. Taking a shaky breath, she drew back, and so did he, one centimeter at a time.

He was the first to find his voice. "As tempting as it is to take a little detour here, I'm not going to."

"You're not?"

He shook his head. "You have my word."

"Oh. Um. Good." Since his word was something she doubted he gave lightly, she led the way through a narrow hallway, past the storage room and restrooms, and into the cavernous tavern in need of paint and a good scrubbing and a brand-new image. Flipping on light switches as she went, she continued until she reached the ornately carved bar where she'd left the box she'd started filling with Lacey's cameras.

"Here's the thing," Reed declared, using her exact terminology.

It occurred to Ruby that he was not a man of almosts. He wasn't almost tall or almost handsome or almost proud. He was all those things and more. He'd drawn a line in the sand and apparently he intended to make certain she knew exactly how far, how deep and how wide the line ran.

"The baby you saw my brother carrying before lunch?" he said.

"Joey?" she asked, standing on tiptoe to reach the last three cameras on the top shelf.

"Joey, yes. You assumed Marsh is his father."

She stood mute, waiting for him to continue.

"Unless I'm mistaken, you alluded to that at the restaurant," he said.

Half the lights in the room were burned out and the bulbs in the other half were so dim and the fixtures so grimy, light didn't begin to reach into the corners. Murky shadows pooled beneath the small tables and mismatched chairs. The billiards tables in the back were idle, the shape of the neatly folded bedroll barely discernible from here.

Carefully tucking Bubble Wrap around another

camera, Ruby finally said, "Are you telling me Marsh isn't Joey's father?"

"It's possible he is." Reed's voice was deep, reverent almost, and extraordinarily serious. "But it's also possible I am."

Surely Ruby's dismay was written all over her face all over again. But she didn't have it in her to care how she looked.

The baby she'd seen before lunch was possibly Reed's? Had she heard him correctly?

"Oh, my God."

He nodded as if he couldn't have said it better himself.

She slid the cumbersome box of cameras aside. Resting one elbow comfortably on the bar's worn surface, she gestured fluidly with her other hand and said, "Have a seat, cowboy. This is one story I've got to hear."

Chapter Four

For years, Bell's Tavern had been considered the black sheep of drinking establishments in Orchard Hill. It was where someone just passing through town went to drink too much and whine to strangers, where regulars and first-timers alike drowned their sorrows and cheated at cards, among other things. Its saving grace had also been its most redeeming quality.

What happened at Bell's Tavern stayed at Bell's Tavern.

It seemed oddly fitting that Reed was about to reveal details of a nearly unbelievable situation to the new owner right here at Bell's, where countless others had undoubtedly done the same thing. Choosing a stool, he sidled up to the bar and made himself comfortable.

The carton containing his sister-in-law's cameras sat on the counter near Ruby's right elbow. As she tucked an old movie projector from the fifties into the box, another curl pulled free of the clip high on the back of her head and softly fluttered to the side of her face. Her skin looked smooth, her lips full and lush, her eyes green and keenly observant.

A warm breeze wafted through the open back door, but other than the muffled sounds of midafternoon meandering in with it, Bell's was quiet and still. And Reed's voice was quiet as he began.

"My brothers and I discovered Joey on our doorstep ten days ago. We heard a noise none of us could identify and rushed out to the front porch. There the baby was, strapped into his car seat, wailing his little head off."

"He was by himself? But he's so small," she said.

Reed released a deep breath. "I know. Who leaves a baby on a doorstep in this day and age? Noah is an airplane test pilot and always buzzes the orchard when he's returning from out of town. From the cab of his plane an hour before we discovered Joey, he saw a woman walking across our front lawn. Despite the fact that it was eighty degrees out that day, she was wearing a dark hooded sweatshirt. We think she was hiding Joey underneath it."

"And you believe this woman was Joey's mother?"

"Who else could she have been?"

When Reed was growing up, his dad always said Marsh and Noah had been born looking up, Marsh to the apple trees and Noah to the sky, while Reed looked at the horizon and the future. That night the three of them had stood dazedly looking down, completely baffled and dumbfounded by the sudden appearance of the baby crying so forlornly at their feet.

"Joey was wearing a blue shirt and only one sock. Days later Noah discovered the other one under the weeping willow tree near the road. We theorize that his mother hid there until we'd taken him safely inside."

Ruby covered her mouth with one hand as if imagining that. If it was true, Joey's mother wasn't someone who'd carelessly and heartlessly dumped her innocent baby off and driven away without a backward glance. Instead, she'd hidden behind a tree where she could see the porch but no one could see her, and had remained there until she was certain Joey was safe.

Reed remembered looking out across their property that evening, past the meadow that would serve as a parking lot that would be teeming with cars in the fall, to the apple trees, gnarled and green, and the neatly mown two-track path between each row. The shed where the parking signs were stored along with the four-wheelers and all the other equipment they used for hayrides and tours every autumn had been closed up tight.

He'd peered at the stand of pines and the huge willow at the edge of the property, but he'd seen nothing out of the ordinary. Certainly no one had moved.

He could only imagine how still she must have held, and he couldn't even fathom how difficult it must have been to leave Joey in such a way. What he didn't know was why. Why had she left him? Why hadn't he or Marsh been told one of them was going to be a father? Why had she waited? Why had it come to this? Why?

"When I picked the baby up, a note fluttered to the porch floor. It said, 'Our precious son, Joseph Daniel Sullivan. He's my life. I beg you take good care of him until I can return for him.'"

Ruby seemed to be waiting for him to continue. When he didn't, she asked, "That's it? That's all the note said?"

Reed nodded. "Nearly word for word. It wasn't addressed or signed. So we don't know which of us is Joey's father." He paused for a moment before clarifying. "It's not what you're thinking."

Tucking another loose curl behind one ear, she said, "You know what I'm thinking?"

"Are you thinking that sounded perverse and oddly twisted?" he asked.

She smiled, and some of the tension that had been building inside him eased. Without explanation, she ducked down behind the bar, disappearing from view. He heard a refrigerator door open below. When she popped back up, she had a bottle of chilled water in each hand.

He accepted the beverage she offered him, and while she opened hers and tipped it up, he thought about that first night with Joey. In five minutes' time, life as he'd known it had gone from orderly to pandemonium.

"Joey was crying and Noah and Marsh were trying to free him from the car seat and I was desperately digging through the bags he'd arrived with until I found feeding supplies. After a few clumsy attempts we managed to prepare a bottle, and while Noah fed Joey, I did a little research online. Judging by his size, the way he made eye contact, supported his own head and kicked his feet and flailed his arms, he was likely three months old, give or take a week or two. We did the math, and reality sank in like a lead balloon. One of the three women from our respective pasts had some explaining to do."

"That's putting it mildly," she said.

He lifted the plastic bottle partway to his mouth and added, "Why would a woman go through a pregnancy alone, physically, financially and emotionally, only to desert a baby as strong and smart and damn close to perfect in every way three months later?"

Ruby shrugged understandingly, and Reed thought she might have missed her calling until now. "Is Lacey the woman from Noah's past?" she asked.

"Yes, she is," Reed said. "She took herself out of the equation almost immediately. Once you've gotten to know Lacey better you'll believe me when I say she wasn't subtle about it, either."

"So," Ruby said gently. "Paternity comes down to you and Marsh."

Reed nodded before taking a long drink of his water. "When you happened upon my near miss this morning, I was on my way home from the drugstore with a paternity test kit. Marsh and I have been interviewing potential nannies all week, but until we find one we both approve of, we're taking turns caring for Joey. Marsh needs to work in the orchard this afternoon, so Joey's going to help me balance the books in the new business system." With that, he pulled the carton of cameras toward him and stood up.

She stepped out from behind the bar and followed, switching lights off along the way. "You two are looking for a nanny for the baby. That's why Marsh practically offered me a job earlier."

"He what?" Reed stopped so abruptly she slammed into him, every lush inch of her front pressing against every solid inch of his back.

Her hands landed on his waist like a pair of fluttery

birds, her breath warm and moist on his shoulder. She was svelte and soft and slender, and if his hands hadn't been busy carrying the cumbersome carton containing Lacey's cameras, there was no telling where he might have put them.

The contact was over quickly, and yet her imprint remained. Heat surged under his skin and need churned in its wake. Heat and need. Man and woman. Hunger and allure.

This was not good.

It felt good, damn good. That wasn't good, either.

"Sorry about that," he said, his voice huskier than it had been moments earlier. "I guess I shouldn't stop in front of you without warning."

An awkward silence stretched like evening shadows. Her cheeks were pink and she didn't seem to know where to look. Reed couldn't stop looking. A vein was pulsing wildly in the little hollow at the base of her neck. One strap of her tank top had slipped off her shoulder again, baring a faint sprinkling of golden freckles he wanted to touch, with his fingertips, and with his lips.

Not good. Not good at all.

Attempting to move his thoughts out of dangerous territory—again—he cleared his throat and said, "You must have made quite an impression on Marsh in order for him to have offered you the position without consulting me."

"At the time," Ruby said on her way once again toward the open door, "I thought it was strange when he asked me if I've ever been arrested or cheated on my taxes or had an overdue library book."

That sounded like his older brother, Reed thought. "Did you accept his offer?"

She made a sound men were hard-pressed to replicate. It was a breathy vibration females learned at a young age. He couldn't see her expression, but he imagined she was rolling her eyes as she said, "Accepting job offers from complete strangers in crowded restaurants is on my bucket list along with picking up hitchhikers, hiking in the woods with serial killers and amputating my toe for fun."

Reed walked outside smiling.

At the threshold of the tavern's back door, she quietly asked, "What about Joey's mother?"

That, he thought, was the million-dollar question. He hoisted the carton of cameras a little higher in his arms and said, "She's either someone I met during a layover in Dallas last year or an artist Marsh fell for on vacation earlier in the same month. Unfortunately, it could take up to four weeks for the paternity test results to be processed and mailed back to us."

"And if she returns in the meantime, as her note implied? What then?" she asked.

"We'd know which of us is his father, wouldn't we?"

"Why did that sound as if you have a plan?" she asked.

Reed was accustomed to feeling unsettled. Feeling understood was new and far too pleasant.

Not good. Not good at all.

"I couldn't hand Joey back to his mother and pretend this never happened. I couldn't forget he exists, and I doubt Marsh could, either."

"You'd fight for custody?" Ruby asked.

Shifting slightly beneath the blazing afternoon sun,

he opened the trunk of the Mustang he was driving until the mirror on his other car was repaired. "If I'm Joey's father, and if Cookie had a good reason for leaving him with no explanation—and it would have to be a very good reason—it's highly likely she'll be in my life. I don't know how this is going to end or what's going to happen between now and then."

Shading her eyes with one hand, she said, "Now isn't a good time for me to lose my direction and it isn't a good time for you to change yours."

"I appreciate the recap."

She pulled a face, but she couldn't help smiling at his wry humor. "Good luck, Reed. I hope you find what you're looking for."

"I prefer not to rely on luck." He closed the trunk and strode to his door. "We've hired the most successful P.I. in the state. And by the way—" he turned back toward the bar and pointed "—we're keeping our eyes open for the young woman Lacey and Noah saw climbing out the tavern's window."

"What?" Ruby yelped. "What woman? What window?" Her voice rose in pitch and volume with every query.

She swung around and looked where he was pointing. Until this instant she hadn't given the window in the loft space above the tavern more than a passing thought. A pipe that had once served as a downspout ran alongside the window all the way to the roof. The pipe had been cut off at some point in time and capped six feet above the ground. The bottom of the window itself was at least fifteen feet up. "You're telling me a woman was seen climbing down the downspout outside my window?"

"Technically it wasn't your window at the time."

She didn't need to tell him this wasn't funny. He wasn't laughing. In fact, he looked dead serious.

"Who was she? What was she doing here? And why would she have been climbing through a second-story window of a derelict building regardless of who owned it at the time?"

Reed reached inside his car and snagged a pair of sunglasses off the dash. Slipping them on, he said, "I suppose because there's no other access to the loft anymore."

She shot him a look that had maimed lesser men.

"Seriously," he said. "Lacey and Noah didn't recognize her, but evidently a few days earlier, Lacey had discovered a sleeping bag under one of the pool tables at Bell's."

A sleeping bag? A gong was going off in Ruby's skull. "But why?" she asked. "What does that have to do with—"

"Apparently someone had been sleeping downstairs in the tavern."

The temperature on the thermometer across the alley registered eighty-seven degrees. That meant Ruby's goose bumps had another origin.

"Lacey called the police," Reed explained. "During a thorough inspection, the officer discovered a water bottle with a pink lipstick stain on the rim under one of the pool tables where the bedroll had been. It's possible whoever stowed the items there was a college student or a runaway. The police have no reason to believe she's still in the area."

"Then she's long gone?" Ruby didn't think she'd ever met a man who held so still, and it occurred to her, as her hand fell away from her eyes, that his stillness was a prelude, like the calm before the storm.

"That's their theory," he said.

"But not necessarily yours," Ruby said, calming down.

"She was sleeping here," she said, thinking out loud. "And the sleeping bag is still here. I'm more interested in your theory than theirs."

"Honestly? I think she'll be back, if not to retrieve the sleeping bag, then for whatever she came to Orchard Hill to do."

"Could she have been Joey's mother?" Ruby asked.

"The women my brother and I were involved with are in their early thirties," he replied. "Lacey thought this girl was closer to seventeen or eighteen, and had light brown hair down to her waist. I don't believe in coincidence, either, and the fact is, Lacey discovered that sleeping bag the same night my brothers and I discovered Joey on our doorstep."

Her unease evaporated like dew in morning sunshine. What did she have to be afraid of, really, except a teenage girl with waist-length hair and a penchant for trespassing?

Ruby had taken self-defense classes in college, although admittedly her best training had begun in childhood. Growing up with a tyrannical twin brother had taught her to recover quickly from surprise attacks around corners, and of course, the sweet art of retaliation.

Operating one of her father's tow trucks hadn't been without risk, either. Now, in purchasing Bell's, she had inadvertently inherited a mystery, and a very puzzling one at that. But she wouldn't let that scare her and get in the way of her plans.

Reed slid behind his steering wheel and started his car. "I appreciate you boxing up Lacey's cameras. Knowing her, she'll stop over and thank you in person when she and Noah get home from their honeymoon next week." With that, he drove away, one arm resting on his lowered window. There was a hint of reluctance in his wave.

Ruby retraced her footsteps inside, where she made a wide sweep of the tavern's interior. At the billiards table where the plush sleeping bag was folded neatly, she went perfectly still, listening for phantom footsteps overhead.

A fly must have followed her in and was buzzing from one light fixture to another. Otherwise, the room was utterly quiet. There were no suspicious creaks, no hollow thuds or discordant scrapes of a window being opened or closed, no footsteps of any kind. In fact, the only other sound in the tavern was the slow release of the breath she'd been holding.

She took one last look at the bedroll on the pool table and locked the back door. As she started up her stairs, she reminded herself that the police didn't expect the young woman to return.

The former owner did, though. And so did Reed Sullivan.

At four-thirty on Friday, Ruby was settled comfortably in a booth at the Hill with a glass of ice-cold lemonade near her left hand, her iPad and phone in front of her and an order of appetizers due any minute from the kitchen.

She'd been in all-systems-go mode since early yesterday. So far she'd hired a father/son duo to refinish the floors and paint the tavern's ceilings, scheduled the electrician, taken applications from two college students with experience waiting tables and arranged to interview a bartender from Lansing. She'd spoken with dozens of people. Many were men. Some were tall. Her toes hadn't tingled once.

Absently sipping her lemonade, she reminded herself that she wasn't going to think about her tingling toes. She wasn't going to think about Reed Sullivan's puzzling situation or how lean and fit he'd felt during those brief moments when her body had been pressed against his. She especially wasn't going to think about that.

She had plenty to occupy her mind, as well as every moment of her time: namely, preparing for Bell's grand reopening three weeks from tonight. Thanks to the little inheritance her grandmother had left her, she'd been able to pay cash for the building. Ruby was a saver from way back—her mother claimed all the O'Tooles still had their first nickel, and she had the money for the renovations and a year's expenses in her savings account. That didn't mean she planned to burn through it. The sooner she had the tavern up and running the better.

She'd missed lunch, and right now, those appetizers she'd ordered were vying for her attention, too. She took another sip through her straw and looked around. Other than a large group seated around a long table in the back of the room, she and a handful of others had the restaurant to themselves. It was the ideal atmosphere to work through dinner.

She drained her lemonade and reviewed the order form she was filling out from a local winery. Prices were high, and although there was a column for unforeseen costs written into the budget, she knew she had to expect hidden expenses.

She *wasn't* expecting a woman with dark hair and a dozen bangles on her wrist to slip uninvited into her booth. Tall and slender, the woman hunkered down slightly in her seat directly opposite Ruby as if trying to make herself as small as possible. Her dress was black and sleeveless, her violet eyes expertly made up, her fingernails as polished as the rest of her. "If you don't move an inch," she said, "dinner is on me."

Ruby had to fight the temptation to look over her shoulder. *"That,"* she said, "is the second-best offer I've had today. Ex-boyfriend?"

"God, no. I'm a wedding planner and that group in the back is here for the rehearsal dinner. I'm finished for the day, but a few minutes ago I was going over a last-minute detail with the bride. Her brother squeezed my, ah, shall we say, derriere? Luckily, his fiancée wasn't looking. This time. My client has been dreaming of her perfect wedding day her whole life, so I think I'll wait until after the cake is cut tomorrow to make a scene. But enough about me. What was your best offer of the day?"

Ruby slanted the woman a secretive smile and said nothing. After a moment the brunette smiled, too.

"I'm Chelsea Reynolds."

"Ruby O'Toole."

"I know. You bought Lacey Bell's tavern. Three nights ago she and Noah Sullivan eloped before flying off into the wild blue yonder. You drive a sky-blue

Chevy and yesterday you were seen talking to the other two Sullivan brothers in the lobby here."

Being careful not to lean forward as she reeled from sheer surprise, and thereby give Chelsea's position away, Ruby said, "What did I have for breakfast?"

Two perfectly shaped eyebrows rose like crescent moons as Chelsea said, "If you give me a minute, I could find out."

Ruby found herself laughing out loud.

With an answering smile, Chelsea said, "I heard Marsh and Reed brought the baby to lunch with them yesterday. Everybody's talking about it. First, Noah elopes, and now, either Marsh or Reed is a father? Women all over Orchard Hill are crying in their beer, which will be good for your business. And if Marsh or Reed wind up planning a wedding, it'll be good for my business. By the way, thanks for allowing me a little cooling-off time-out at your table."

"You're welcome," Ruby said.

"Why did you?" Chelsea asked.

Watching a bead of condensation trail down the side of her glass, Ruby said, "A few months ago I ducked behind the produce stand at Meijer when my ex-boyfriend came into the store."

"Did he see you?" Chelsea asked.

"I'm afraid so," Ruby said. "Evidently being among the last to know he was a lying two-timing flea-ridden hound dog wasn't humiliating enough."

Chelsea stopped brushing invisible lint from the front of her dress and sneered. "If he shows up in Orchard Hill, let me know. I have extremely sharp knee-caps, or, if need be, a fantabulous pair of pointy-toed Jimmy Choo knockoffs."

Ruby would have to keep that in mind, although she wasn't worried Peter would show his face in Orchard Hill. He was just conceited enough to believe she would come crawling back to him. She really had thought she loved him. Now she dreaded seeing him at the class reunion, and hoped he didn't embarrass her further.

"Jimmy Choo knockoffs?" she said. "Be still my heart."

"I know," Chelsea agreed. "It's all about being in the right place at the right time."

The stuffed mushrooms and mozzarella sticks arrived piping hot and smelling like heaven, and while Chelsea and Ruby compared dating horror stories, another place setting was brought out, another order for dinner placed, and cheating men and fitting retaliations discussed and diabolically plotted. For the next hour and a half, Ruby left her iPad off, silenced her cell phone and simply enjoyed Chelsea Reynolds's wry humor and quick wit.

"Tell me about the new Bell's," Chelsea said as she dipped her breadstick in marinara sauce.

And Ruby launched into her favorite topic these days: her vision for her tavern. "Think upscale pub meets back-alley brewery. There will be cards in the back, billiards tournaments the first Friday of every month, fun, noise and laughter. And, of course, dancing on weekends."

Spearing a wedge of tomato in her salad, Chelsea said, "There's nothing like hot and loud to work up a thirst and keep the drink orders coming."

"There is that," Ruby agreed. "It's so much more than a business venture to me. I want Bell's to be a place people come to have fun, a place where someone goes to celebrate finally turning twenty-one or where coworkers meet at the end of a long week. I'd like it to be a stop for soon-to-be brides having one last hurrah with the girls before marrying the man of their dreams. Who knows? Couples might even meet for the first time there, and maybe fall in love. I hope people have a good time at my new place regardless of why they stop in, and when they need it, a chance to sulk or brood."

Sometime after their entrée dishes were cleared away and their desserts ordered, Chelsea reached into her bag and brought out a sketch pad. Animated and invigorated by the opportunity to talk about her tavern, Ruby was only vaguely aware of the jangle of bracelets as Chelsea made wide sweeps across the paper with her pencil.

They talked about the renovations she was making and the one-of-a-kind drinks she planned to offer. Chelsea loved Kerfuffle and Dynamite and Starstruck. She suggested Cheater Beater, which was similar to Ruby's brother's suggestion, Ball Buster, both of which Ruby thought she'd pass on. But Chelsea was easy to talk to, and just as easy to listen to.

Finally, there was a lull in the conversation, and they both pushed their half-eaten desserts away. Chelsea tore the top sheet of paper from her sketch pad and with a flourish held it out to Ruby.

Taking it, Ruby could only stare in wonder at the whimsical sketch. "You're an artist?"

"I'm not trained professionally, but I can't help myself sometimes. This is your personal little welcome to Orchard Hill."

The waitress arrived with the check and foam boxes

for leftovers, and soon Ruby and Chelsea wended their way through the crowd now filling the restaurant's lobby. Outside, Chelsea unlocked a shiny black Audi, and Ruby veered into the first alleyway she came to. She had her oversize bag on one shoulder, an amazing sketch advertising Bell's grand reopening tucked away neatly inside. She also had an invitation to dinner tomorrow night circling the back of her mind, and a new friend. Not one of those had been on her to-do list, which proved once again that sometimes the best things in life simply happened.

She strode east, then north and east again through the alleys that crisscrossed the business district of Orchard Hill. Smiling at dog walkers, kids on bikes and couples out for an evening stroll, she didn't give the route she took more than a passing thought. She didn't need to. Her sense of direction was once again in perfect working order. Obviously yesterday had been a fluke.

Feeling hopeful about the future and happy about today, she rounded the final corner and instantly saw a girl coming toward her.

They both veered slightly, effortlessly averting an awkward collision, Ruby's red hair swishing around her shoulders and the girl's waist-length hair swishing around hers. Ruby smiled, but the girl only gave her a curt nod in return. Without so much as slowing down, she continued on her way.

Ruby stared after her, her heart thudding. The sight of a teenage girl with long hair and a T-shirt emblazoned with the words Beethoven Rocks was no cause for alarm, and yet Ruby was seriously considering following her. It had nothing to do with the girl's hair or her clothing or even her dancer's gait, and everything to do with the pink-and-green bedroll tucked beneath her arm.

She didn't look back. Ruby watched to make sure. After the girl had disappeared around the first corner she came to, Ruby ran to the tavern's back door, unlocked it and threw it wide open.

She knew what she would find, but she turned on lights and hurried to the pool table, anyway. The sleeping bag was gone, just as she'd expected.

Ruby thought about everything Reed had told her about his situation and its possible connection to the girl Lacey and Noah had seen climbing from the window outside Ruby's back door. She could only imagine how shocking it must have been to discover a baby on their doorstep, and to realize that one of them was little Joey's father. Reed had most likely barely scratched the surface when he'd mentioned what they were doing to care for Joey and the steps they were taking to locate the baby's mother.

He'd been right about one thing. The girl certainly wasn't a figment of anyone's imagination. Ruby had seen her with her own two eyes. She appeared to be in her late teens and she was definitely still in Orchard Hill. Apparently she was still letting herself in and out of the tavern without the use of a key, too.

Was her presence here in Orchard Hill connected to little Joey Sullivan's, as Reed suspected? How could it be, and if so, what possible connection could there be between a girl letting herself in and out of Ruby's bar and one little baby boy?

It was a puzzle, and yet, Ruby felt strongly that Reed was right. It seemed unlikely that these puzzling coincidences weren't somehow related in some profound way. How remained a mystery, and yet, reaching into her shoulder bag for her car keys, she knew what she had to do.

Chapter Five

"You two are killin' me here. You know that, right?" the P.I. asked as he rummaged through a coffee-stained file folder.

Reed and Marsh both shrugged. Sam Lafferty had arrived at their door fifteen minutes ago in faded jeans and an impossibly wrinkled shirt. His red-rimmed eyes and gruff attitude hadn't fooled either of them. Sam may have been short on sleep and long on dead ends, but he had the stealth of a leopard on the scent of an antelope.

Wherever Joey's mother was, *whoever* Joey's mother was, he would find her. That knowledge—no, that *faith*—made it a little easier to sleep at night for both Sullivan brothers.

"I have another photo here I want you to look at,"

Sam said. "Where the hell did it go? I saw it a minute ago. I'm sure of it."

Reed felt the man's sense of urgency. Times ten.

They'd begun this evening's meeting seated around the iron-and-glass patio table outside. It hadn't taken Joey long to drink his bottle and it hadn't taken Reed long to grow restless. Putting the baby to his shoulder for a burp, he'd risen to his feet. Now all three men stood in a semicircle in the dappled shade near the back door.

It was that time of the day when sounds seemed to carry for miles. Insects buzzed and a television perpetually tuned to the weather droned faintly through the open window. An airplane rumbled above the clouds and every once in a while another car could be heard pulling away from the stop sign on the corner. Much, much closer, Joey made mewling sounds against Reed's shoulder.

Reed had a keen business sense, always had, and yet he could set his clock by the length and angle of the shadows in the orchard. All four of the Sullivan siblings could. On this, the first official day of summer, sunset was still another two and a half hours away. Even then, darkness would creep slowly from one horizon to the other, gathering in doorways and around corners before saturating the very air between the earth and the sky.

Not long ago Reed had had that kind of patience. Now he wanted action. He wanted answers. And he wanted both right now.

"Here it is," Sam said, handing over the print he'd been looking for. "Take a look at this one, Reed."

Sam had been searching for Joey's mother for ten days now. To Reed, it felt like much longer. The P.I.

had conducted dozens of internet searches and personal searches, had sat through tedious hours of surveillance and had followed leads to North Carolina, Tennessee and Texas. He'd been kicked, punched and threatened, but insisted it was all in a day's work. He'd spoken with the owners of the little shops and coffeehouses Marsh and Julia had visited on the Outer Banks last year, and he'd also made a pass through every little restaurant within a five-mile radius of the Dallas airport where Reed had met a waitress named Cookie a few weeks later.

Sam had called in favors and had forwarded to Reed and Marsh pictures of women who might potentially be Joey's mother doing everything from shopping to running a red light. "Does the stacked little blonde in that photo look at all familiar?" he asked.

Keeping one hand on Joey's back, Reed studied the image carefully. The woman in the photograph had shoulder-length blond hair and plenty of it. Texas hair, Cookie had called it.

"It was taken at a crosswalk on a busy street in downtown Dallas yesterday," Sam explained. "Until seven months ago, she worked at a restaurant near the airport."

Reed continued to study the image. In the photo, her head was turned slightly away from the camera, showcasing her profile. Could this be her?

He'd racked his brain trying to remember every detail about their brief encounter last year. "The woman I knew was blonde and nice-looking. She had a great body, but I don't remember her being quite this chesty."

"Have you ever seen a woman who's been breastfeeding? If you haven't, you need to," Sam insisted.

"Trust me, if Cookie had a baby, she'd likely be even more stacked. Does it look like her, otherwise?"

Even in heels, the woman in the photo was shorter than the people she was with, just like the flustered waitress who'd accidentally spilled chili in Reed's lap last year. This woman's height was right, her hair was right, the clothes were right, the city was right. "I suppose it could be her," he said.

"Shoot me some odds," Sam grumbled.

"It's possible. I don't know beyond that," Reed said. "What else do you know about the woman in this photo?"

"She's twenty-nine, works as a sales clerk at a department store and recently began a new job moonlighting at a restaurant that just opened up downtown. Her name is Bobby Jean Pritchard, but according to my source, her friends call her Corky. Occasionally she goes by Cookie. God knows, Texans like their nicknames. Why don't you tell Uncle Sam here what pet name she had for you."

The sound Reed made through his clenched teeth was as uncouth as he would allow himself to be with the baby in his arms. Sam chuckled. Marsh's curiosity must have finally gotten the better of him, for he took the photo when Reed was finished and looked, too.

Reed had told Sam all the pertinent information he could recall from his encounter with Cookie last year. She'd waited on him at a little café near the airport. When the bowl of chili he'd ordered slid off her tray and landed upside down on his table, thick red globs dropping onto his lap, her eyes had widened in genuine horror. She'd apologized over and over and started dabbing up chili with paper napkins. He'd stopped her before she'd done any real damage.

She said her name was Cookie, that she was single and had been born and raised in Dallas. She'd had what sounded like a genuine Texas accent and wore a ring on her little finger, more than one bracelet, big hoop earrings and clothes that were tight in all the right places.

Attractive and a little pushy, she was the one who'd suggested they go someplace more private when her shift was over. Reed certainly hadn't objected. They'd taken his rental car to her place. It seemed to him that her apartment building had been only a mile or two from the restaurant. This was one instance when an eidetic memory would have come in handy, for the apartment complex had looked like hundreds of other apartment complexes. She'd had the usual furniture, a small television, a few framed photographs, potted plants on a low table and shoes scattered about.

Had Joey been conceived in a nondescript apartment beneath a noisy window air conditioner? The idea chafed. They'd used protection, but every man alive knew that only abstinence had an unwritten guarantee.

Joey wiggled at Reed's shoulder the way he always did when he needed to burp but couldn't. Patting his little back as if it was second nature, Reed couldn't help thinking that the encounter that produced this amazing little kid should have been more memorable. But berating himself wasn't doing any good. It wouldn't be the first time a child had been born as a result of a one-night stand and it probably wouldn't be the last. That didn't ease his sore conscience, however.

He and Cookie had both been adults, and they'd both known what they were doing. Neither of them had done a lot of talking after they'd reached her place. Now he wished he would have at least thought to ask her real name. It was a shame he hadn't saved the heart-shaped note she'd tucked into his pants pocket hours later, for on it she'd written her phone number in bright pink ink.

Joey finally burped, and it was unbelievably loud for someone so small. Even Sam, who insisted he didn't know one end of a baby from the other, couldn't help smiling.

"What else can you tell us?" Reed asked the P.I.

"Before I left Dallas," Sam said, closing the file folder on the table, "I had a guy I know run the note you found the night you discovered the baby. He lifted five partial sets of fingerprints. Four came from men with big hands." He held up his bear paw. "Mine, and since all three of you Sullivan brothers handled the note, it stands to reason your prints would be on it, too. The fifth set was smaller, definitely female."

"And?" Reed and Marsh prodded in unison.

"Her prints aren't on file with the police. It appears our girl doesn't have a record, which is good for her but another dead end for us. I had another friend analyze the handwriting, the ink and the paper."

Reed and Marsh were so intent upon what Sam was telling them that they paid little attention to the light blue car slowly coming up their driveway. Maybe they'd get lucky and this new information would be the breakthrough they'd been waiting for. Hopefully it would lead them to the woman who'd left Joey on their doorstep seemingly out of the blue less than two weeks ago.

"Was Julia Monroe right- or left-handed?" Sam asked Marsh, his gaze flickering to the driveway.

"Right-handed."

Sam looked at Reed next. "What about Cookie?"

Reed recalled the way Cookie had slowly torn his receipt from her order pad that night, and later scribbled her phone number on a small piece of paper. "She was right-handed, too," he said. "What did the handwriting analysis reveal?"

"Plain white stationery, blue ink, a steady, flowing script written in a woman's right hand. Now, which one of you is holding out on me?"

"What are you talking about?" Marsh groused.

"The question you should be asking isn't what," Sam insisted. "It's who. As in, who's the redhead?"

Reed finally took a good look at the sky-blue Chevy pulling to a stop behind Sam's dusty Ford. The next thing he knew, the driver's-side door was opening and Ruby O'Toole was getting out.

There were three men standing near the sprawling white house when Ruby parked behind a dented SUV with a Michigan license plate. All three were tall, and all three watched her so intently as she approached she had to fight the temptation to smooth her skirt and fiddle with her bracelet.

Reed was holding Joey and talking with Marsh and a man she didn't recognize. Judging by their squared shoulders and serious expressions, she'd interrupted something important.

"You were right, Reed," she said, getting directly to the point the instant she reached the patio. "That girl with the long hair is still in Orchard Hill."

"How do you know?" Reed asked.

"I saw her."

His brow furrowed as he said, "When?"

"A little while ago in the alley outside my place. She returned for the bedroll, just like you thought she would."

The slight breeze sifted through Reed's short blond hair, and a shadow darkened his jaw. Joey wiggled, his head bobbing as he looked at something over Reed's shoulder.

"Are you two talking about the girl who was sleeping in the tavern?" Marsh cut in.

Ruby started. Oh. Right. There were others present.

"Yes," she said to the darker-haired Sullivan. "I came face-to-face with her while I was walking home from dinner not more than half an hour ago."

"You're sure it was her?" Marsh asked.

"I'm pretty sure, yes."

As if trying to piece together her impromptu encounter with the mysterious girl, Reed said, "You mentioned that she returned for the bedroll. Did you actually see the sleeping bag?"

"It was tucked under her arm. I was pretty sure it was the same one. The moment she was out of sight, I ran to the tavern and checked. The bedroll Lacey asked me to leave out was gone. You told me you thought this girl's presence in Orchard Hill was somehow related to Joey's, so I drove right over."

His tired smile caught her unawares, stirring something in that secret place beneath her breastbone where forgotten dreams lay waiting. Although the patio was shaded, heat lingered in the flagstones beneath the soles of her sandals. Surely that was where this warmth originated.

"Reed," the man she hadn't met said. "Maybe you

could do the honors. And somebody bring me up to date here."

Reed's eyes widened for a moment, but when he spoke, it was with efficient practicality. "This is Sam Lafferty, Ruby, the P.I. helping us locate Joey's mother. Sam, Ruby O'Toole."

She and Sam Lafferty forewent a formal handshake as they sized each other up. So he was a private investigator, she thought. She might have guessed that from his appearance, although he could just as easily have been a bouncer or an undercover cop or a fugitive, for that matter.

Close to six-four in his scuffed boots, he stood with his feet apart, muscles flexed, hips slightly forward in the cocksure manner of a man who was confident in his sex appeal and wanted everyone to know it. She'd known men like that. In fact, she'd fancied herself having a future with one, but that was before she'd discovered Peter had been cheating on her.

Never again.

To his credit, Sam Lafferty's gaze didn't slip below her shoulders. She cut him a little slack for good behavior and followed his gaze to the table where a thick file lay near an empty baby bottle.

"Walk us through the encounter," he said. "From the beginning, if you wouldn't mind."

"Of course," she replied. "I've been exploring the alleyways that run behind the businesses lining Division Street, familiarizing myself with the stores and shops while testing my sense of direction, you might say." She happened to glance at Reed. Once again, it wasn't easy to look away. "I rounded a corner and came face-to-face with the girl."

"Can you describe her?" the P.I. asked.

"She was around five foot six, had an oval face, blue eyes and brown hair down to her waist. I didn't see any piercings, but there was a butterfly tattoo on the inside of her right wrist. Her bag was Coach and her sandals had cork heels. And she had the sleeping bag under her left arm."

"How long did this encounter last?" Sam Lafferty asked.

She pondered a moment, considering. "She didn't stick around long. We were probably walking toward one another no more than five or six seconds."

"That's a lot of detail to recall after only five or six seconds," he pointed out.

It was Reed who explained, "Ruby has an eidetic memory." At Sam's raised eyebrows, he said, "Do a Google search. Better yet, she'd probably recite your license plate number if you asked nice."

She rattled off the number effortlessly, her gaze never straying from the unkempt P.I.'s.

Sam's surprise was almost comical. He recovered quickly, though, and said, "How old would you say this girl was?"

"Late teens most likely. I seriously think twenty would be a stretch. She wasn't at all what I would expect someone who sleeps in derelict buildings and climbs out of second-story windows to look like. She seemed polished. Poised. She must have nerves of steel because she didn't glance over her shoulder as she hurried away, although I sensed she knew I was watching her. There's one more thing."

She turned to Reed and Marsh. "She was wearing

a silver chain around her neck and a monogrammed charm. I'm pretty sure two of the initials were J and S."

"Joseph Sullivan," Reed said.

She found herself looking at the baby. His little T-shirt was bunched slightly beneath Reed's hand, exposing the top of his diaper and the unbelievably soft-looking skin on his lower back. His feet were bare, his dark wispy hair standing adorably on end. It was hard to imagine anyone abandoning a child so innocent, so small and healthy in every way.

Silence stretched and the mood became even more somber. The clues were stacking up, and they all indicated that the girl with the long hair was indeed connected in some profound way to Joey and this case, although at this point the actual nature of the connection was pure speculation. Was she a family member, someone who was somehow related to Joey's mother and consequently Joey, too? Or was she a close friend? What did she know? Why was she here in Orchard Hill? And where was the baby's mother?

Questions abounded. Eventually they would be answered. They had to be. But when?

Since Ruby had relayed everything she'd come here to say, she backed up a step, preparing to leave. "You three undoubtedly have important matters to discuss."

"Thank you," Marsh said, his voice deep and moving. "For taking the time to drive out here and for going to the trouble to try to help. Would you care for something to drink before you head back? A Pepsi or a cold beer? I don't know about you, but I could use a nice neat scotch."

She laughed unconsciously. "Thanks, but I'm meeting someone later. I'll have something then." With a nod at all three, she began the short walk to her car.

Reed didn't stop to analyze his actions as he fell into step beside Ruby. He simply matched his stride to hers. His shoulder was close to hers, their elbows nearly touching. Their shadows glided ahead of them over the grass, her skirt airy and her long red hair curly and free.

This late in the day, the shade from the maple tree his great-grandfather had planted the day after he returned from World War One stretched across the driveway. Joey had been fitful earlier, but now he was completely relaxed, his little head turned so that his cheek rested on Reed's shoulder, his body completely supported in Reed's arms.

Being careful not to jostle the baby, Reed stopped in the fringe of dappled shade, reached around Ruby and opened her door. "That's twice you've gone above and beyond the call of duty and twice all I have to offer is my gratitude."

"Gratitude-smatitude," she replied, wrinkling her nose.

There was something appealing about her irreverence. It wasn't the first time he'd noticed. "You're uncommonly kind, Ruby."

Her smile was wide and genuine, her bottom teeth just crowded enough to make it unlike anyone else's. He took a deep breath, and caught a hint of flowery perfume. He hadn't been expecting that any more than he was expecting her to reach her hand toward him. He thought she meant to touch him, but she laid her hand gently on Joey's back, instead.

"He looks safe and secure in your arms, Reed, as if he knows he's home."

The simple observation touched him most of all.

She got in the car, adjusted her skirt and fastened her seat belt. "Good night. And good luck," she said.

As she was driving away, he wondered who she was having drinks with later. Not that it mattered. It didn't, not in the least. He was curious, that was all.

Very curious.

Marsh and Sam were looking at him when he returned to the patio. Reed wanted to wipe the smug expressions off both their faces.

"My Sunday school teacher had it all wrong," Sam exclaimed.

"Leave it alone, Sam," Marsh warned.

"You went to Sunday school?" Reed asked.

"You're missing my point," the big man with the attitude to match declared.

"Maybe you should make your point," Reed said, his voice so gravelly Joey stirred in his arms. "Are you on the clock?"

"Prickly, aren't you?" Sam quipped. "It's no skin off my nose what you do, or who, for that matter. It's just that it occurred to me that maybe the Garden of Eden was an orchard not a jungle. Apples and temptation seem to go hand in hand." He cast a pointed look at the apple trees nearby. "Reed, I'd lay nine to one odds that your life is about to get even more complicated. For the record, that observation was a freebie. The kid's asleep. Do you want to put him in bed before or after I tell you what lead I'm following next?"

Reed gritted his teeth. Remorse didn't sit well with

him. Tightening his arms protectively around the baby, he said, "What's next? Fire away."

And without further ado, Sam did.

The stars were out.

Reed had watched them flicker into view one by one. Normally he wasn't much of a stargazer, but he'd been out here for a while. Brooding. Berating himself.

He could see the lights in Orchard Hill from here. A mile and a half away, the tallest building downtown was four stories high. When September rolled around, the football field would be lit up like a space station every Friday night. The brightest streetlights lined the business district; the rest of the city stretched out beneath the softer glow of streetlamps on every corner. It was a far cry from an urban skyline.

Reed put the plastic bottle to his lips and let the cool water run down his throat. Why was he sitting here in the dark? Why had he let Sam get to him? Why seemed to be the question tonight.

He leaned back in his chair and stared at the lights in the distance. At last count, there were twenty-five thousand people living in Orchard Hill. Technically twenty-five thousand was a high number, but compared to Chicago or Baltimore or Seattle, this was a small town. Once upon a time, he'd been certain he would spend his entire adult life in one of those cities. He'd certainly never planned to come back to the family orchard. To visit, sure, but not to live.

The Orchard O's varsity basketball team had taken state's his senior year. As the starting center, he'd been offered a sports scholarship from a big-ten college downstate. Reed didn't have the passion or the desire or, truth be told, the talent to be a professional athlete, and he'd known it. He'd had something else in mind, and Purdue came through with an academic scholarship. The following September he had been on his way toward an eventual MBA and an urban lifestyle that included a different restaurant every night and elevators to the twenty-eighth floor.

Then Marsh's phone call had come one cold February afternoon. His voice as hollow as an echo, he'd said there had been an accident. Either Marsh had stopped speaking in complete sentences after that, or Reed only heard every other word. An icy pileup on the interstate. Twenty miles from home. Their parents. Killed instantly. Both of them. Gone. Just gone.

Reed had returned to Purdue after the funeral, and he'd remained on the dean's list and the debate team and in all the right clubs for promising young professionals. He could have stayed the course he'd set because Marsh, then nearly twenty-three years old, had stepped into the role of head of the family, becoming guardian to Noah and Madeline, both just weeks away from their sixteenth and thirteenth birthdays respectively.

But Reed's course had been changed instantly and irrevocably by a force no mortal could fully comprehend. He'd doubled his class load and hurriedly finished his degree. He'd followed a new course, for he'd discovered a need for something deeper than a concrete skyline and an elevator to the twenty-eighth floor.

He'd come home and never regretted it. For Reed, it had become a point of pride. In the years since, he'd rarely thought about that old urban dream. He certainly never considered moving to Seattle or Baltimore anymore. Instead of living in some loft or high-rise, he'd moved back to the sprawling white house where he'd grown up. Together, he and Marsh had finished raising Noah and Madeline. With hard work, careful planning, educated risks and a little luck, they'd expanded the family orchard into the business it was today. Reed wasn't rich, but his life counted. That thirst for something that was missing had never quite been quenched, though.

Until the night Joey arrived.

He scrubbed a hand over his eyes. Earlier he'd done some work in his office off the living room after Sam left. Unable to concentrate, he'd brought his laptop out here only to close it before the first stars appeared. He'd heard Joey crying briefly earlier. By now Marsh had most likely tucked him into the crib they'd assembled together a few days after they'd discovered him on this very porch.

The screen door creaked open. Relying on moonlight and the light spilling through the living room window, Marsh joined him on the porch, a bottle of water in his hand. Two weeks ago they would have both been having a beer about now.

"Joey asleep?" Reed asked.

"Yeah." Marsh sat down, his forearms resting on his thighs, the bottle held loosely in both hands. Reed knew that pose. Whatever he had on his mind was important. Looking at the sky, Reed thought it was possible the stars would burn out while he waited for Marsh to speak. Thankfully he didn't have to wait quite that long.

Finally, he began. "Twice now I've seen the way

you reacted when you came within ten feet of Ruby O'Toole."

Silence.

Marsh unscrewed the cap and tipped the bottle up, then lowered it again. "I noticed you didn't deny it."

Reed didn't waste his breath telling Marsh he was making too much of this.

"I know how you feel." Marsh's voice was barely more than a dusky whisper, but full of conviction. "It's like holding Great-granddad's divining rods too close to a power line. The buzz paralyzes you, but not quite everywhere."

Reed could have done without the analogy, even though it described the sensation fairly accurately. "Was that how it was when you met Julia?" he asked.

Marsh made a reluctant sound that meant yes. "I know you want Joey to be your son. And you know I'm hoping he's mine. We haven't talked about it, but we're handling it. We always do. That said, in a perfect world, he would wind up mine, not because I'd be a better father than you. He'd be mine because that would mean his mother is the woman I fell in love with at first sight last summer."

Reed couldn't fault Marsh for the insinuation that it would be better somehow if Joey were the product of something more meaningful than a one-night stand. He'd thought the same thing. That didn't change anything, however.

"I thought Julia felt the same way about me, and yet once the week was over, she never returned my calls. I tried for weeks. I assumed she didn't want to talk to me. What else could I think? Still, if I were in charge of a perfect world, Joey would be mine," Marsh said after taking another swig of his water. "And Mom and Dad would be the ones sitting on this porch and Madeline wouldn't have had to go through the hell she went through last year, and those kids from Lakewood wouldn't have drowned in Lake Michigan last month and nobody would die until they were good and ready. But then Madeline wouldn't be happily married and expecting her first child and, hell, I suppose the world would get pretty overpopulated my way."

"You're saying maybe it's best that we can't see the big picture?" Reed asked.

"I wouldn't go that far."

Reed was tempted to smile.

"The fact is," Marsh said, "Joey could just as easily be yours as mine. I can't think of anyone, barring myself, who would be better for the job. Either way, we'll both do the right thing because that's who we are."

Reed felt a deep stirring of affection for his brother. They were so different, yet profoundly the same.

"But, Reed? If Cookie, or whatever her name is, is his mother, Ruby O'Toole might just be your Achilles' heel, and by association, mine."

"I'm not some rutting teenager, Marsh. I can handle this. Contrary to what Joey's very existence might indicate, I'm not a prisoner to my hormones."

"Reed? This involves more than hormones. I saw it with my own two eyes. She lights you up. We both know there's a lot at stake here."

Reed took a careful breath. Marsh wasn't telling him anything he didn't know. Monday morning they had another appointment with their great-uncle, Judge Ivan-the-Terrible Sullivan. It wouldn't take much for that contrary old buzzard to decide Joey would be bet-

ter off in foster care than with a couple of single brothers who didn't even know which of them was his father.
The employment agency was sending two more nannies for them to interview on Monday afternoon. They
desperately needed help with Joey's care, but so far no
one they'd interviewed had come close to being good
enough. Until a nanny could be found their time was
divided between Joey's care and work. The trees were
loaded with apples. They needed to be sprayed and
the heaviest branches braced. After last year's devas-
tating spring frost, they needed a good yield, a pros-
perous year.

"There's a lot riding on our shoulders," Marsh insisted.

"You mean on our actions," Reed said.

"And on our *re*actions. Ruby O'Toole is a stunner,
Reed."

Mile-long legs, sparkling green eyes and a gener-
ous smile flashed unbidden into Reed's mind. "She's
uncommonly kind."

"I believe you. It's part of the package that lights
you up. I'm speaking from experience when I say that
kind of electricity isn't easy to resist."

"There's nothing improper between us. I'm resisting just fine."

Marsh raised his bottle. Instead of drinking, he said,
"What we resist persists."

Reed nearly groaned. Their baby sister had gone all
Zen last year. Not Marsh, too.

"It's like floodwater," Marsh explained. "It always
finds the point of entry it seeks."

"Ruby has her own reasons for keeping things light,
Marsh."

"And yet, the zing."

Of the three Sullivan brothers, Marsh was the gruffest and the quietest. At times like this, he was also very, very wise. "What do you suggest?"

"Honestly? I'm hoping you'll remember it's your turn to go for takeout."

The last thing Reed expected to do was laugh, but it rumbled out of him, rusty and real. He and Marsh were two single men who weren't afraid of the washer and dryer, vacuum cleaners, disinfectants and mops. Madeline had liked to cook when she was growing up. When Noah was home between sky events, he'd picked up the slack and fired up the grill. When it was just Marsh and Reed, they invariably ordered out.

"You're saying you're hungry?" Reed asked.

"Is this a day that ends in *y?*"

Feeling lighter somehow, Reed stood up. "A loaded pizza from Murphy's okay with you?"

"Now you're talking."

He recapped his bottle of water and carried it with him to the steps. At the bottom, he said, "Marsh?"

"Yeah?"

"Even if Sam locates Cookie first, even if the results of that paternity test name me as Joey's father, I hope you find Julia. She has to be out there somewhere."

Reed left his brother sitting in the dark with his bottle of purified water, and headed for his Mustang. He had the pizza ordered before he reached the end of the driveway. And he thought about Marsh's maxim.

What we resist persists.

Not only was his older brother wise. In this instance,

he was probably right. By the time Reed passed the city limits sign, he knew what he had to do about Ruby O'Toole and this zing.

Chapter Six

Kissing was in the air tonight.

Ruby glanced delicately at the couple stealing kisses at a nearby table. She needn't have been discreet. They were going at it pretty heavy and wouldn't have noticed if cymbals clanged and lightning struck.

Not that lightning would. It was a beautiful night, the stars faint above the soft glow of outdoor lights, the air mild even now.

She'd chosen this table here in the courtyard at Murphy's because of its clear view of Bell's. Situated on a diagonal across the street, her place was dark tonight, the curbside parking wide-open. That wouldn't be the case for long.

Her two companions were no strangers to Murphy's. In fact, they hadn't been strangers anyplace they'd gone tonight.

"Abby," Chelsea Reynolds said. "I'll give you ten dollars if you go inside and kiss that biker with the red bandanna on his head before he plays 'Shut Up and Kiss Me' one more time. You would be doing humanity a favor if you put him out of all our misery."

Abby Fitzpatrick pushed her short wispy hair behind her ears and said, "If you want the misery to stop, kiss him yourself. He's a little scary for my taste."

"You have taste?" Chelsea asked.

Abby stuck out her tongue at Chelsea, and Ruby thought there was never a dull moment with these two. Longtime friends, they'd arrived at Ruby's hours ago. Petite and blonde, Abby wore tight jeans and amazing heels, the effects of which were wasted since most of the guys she'd encountered hadn't been able to peel their eyes off her chest. Abby was a reporter and office manager at the local newspaper. As lively as a sailor on weekend leave, she believed in having fun.

With her dark hair and violet eyes, Chelsea was lean and lithe, and had forgone jeans entirely for a short black skirt and silk tank. She'd received a lot of looks, too, but her admirers were cautious about it. It was as if the men in Orchard Hill knew any open ogling would bring them pain of one sort or another.

It had been Abby's idea to check out the competition tonight. Located on the third block of Division Street, Drake's had mouthwatering bar burgers, but their service was slow and the majority of their clientele was in the over-fifty category. Like Murphy's, the Whiskey Barrel had found a unique niche. It was on one of the side streets off Division, and was the only place in town with karaoke on Friday nights. Ruby had lost count of how many songs people had sung about kissing. What could she say? Kissing was in the air tonight. Even Chelsea had sung along to "Seven Little Girls Sitting in the Back Seat." Although Murphy's had a full-service bar inside, it was more of a beer-and-pizza place. It was also the most crowded and might just be her biggest competitor. But Ruby was a firm believer in an abundant universe, and wasn't worried about the competition.

From her peripheral vision, she saw a guy wearing cargo shorts and a polo shirt approaching the table. "Hey, Abby," he said, "are you going to introduce me to this tall gorgeous splash of water you brought with you?"

"Why would I do that, Warren?" Abby asked. "She hasn't done anything to me."

Evidently accustomed to Abby's wry humor, he focused on Ruby and cranked up the wattage in his smile. "I haven't gone by Warren since middle school. I'm Ren Colby. Can I buy you a drink?"

It wasn't a bad smile. He wasn't bad-looking, all things considered. Dark hair, decent shoulders, definitely not tall, though. "Thanks, but I'm the designated driver tonight." She jangled the crushed ice in her Diet Coke. "Why don't you stop by Bell's grand reopening in three weeks? If you bring your friends I'll buy *you* a drink."

"I'll do that." He sauntered away, taller suddenly.

Abby shook her head in amazement. "My, you are good. Chelsea's right. You *are* worthy of us. Do you see that guy by the brick wall underneath the speakers?"

"The one with the ponytail or the pirate tattoo?" Ruby asked.

"Ponytail. He wore black-rimmed glasses long before they came back in vogue. I got stuck in an elevator with him once. Long story. He kisses like a cocker spaniel."

"Too much tongue?"

"Would you two mind?" Chelsea grumbled, dropping her pizza crust onto her plate. "I'm trying to eat here."

"Jeez, Chelsea," Abby admonished. "You're a grouch tonight. We really need to find you a man. How about that guy by the door?"

"You can have him," Chelsea said. "You can have them all. Or have you already?"

"Very funny." Abby turned to Ruby. "Don't listen to her. I might kiss and tell, but I don't let just anybody past first base." She stuck out her chest a little. "Gotta protect the girls here, you know? For the record, I haven't kissed every guy here. I haven't kissed Reed."

"Who?" Ruby asked, perhaps just a teensy bit too quickly.

"Reed Sullivan," Abby replied. "He's over by the pizza window. He just got here."

Ruby couldn't help looking over her shoulder. The take-out window was separated from the "drinking" section by thick rope draped between heavy posts. Reed stood on the other side of the divider looking much as he had when she'd driven away earlier, tall and lean and lost in thought. The old-fashioned gaslights turned his hair the color of beach sand and bleached the blue of his shirt nearly white.

Abby sighed. "My sister says no one French-kisses like Reed. The choirboys really are the ones you have to watch. I'm going to the restroom. Anybody care to come along?"

A new song blasted from the speakers and Chelsea made some sort of reply. Ruby had stopped listening. She felt the bump of bass from a passing car, but the courtyard and the world beyond had fallen strangely silent. Her heart beating like a drumroll, she watched Abby and Chelsea stroll leisurely toward the door, which was perhaps ten feet from the window where Reed was now paying for his pizza. Abby must have called to him, because he glanced over his shoulder at them. Their backs were to the street now, and evidently they didn't notice the scooter that was jumping the curb, the single headlight barreling right toward them.

Ruby held her breath, and the next thing she knew, Reed was vaulting over the ropes and hurtling through the air toward the pair directly in the scooter's path. A split second later, Abby and Chelsea were airborne, too.

Ruby reached them moments after they landed on the ground, an iron post crashing down beside them. It fell short, missing them all by mere inches. The scooter and the driver were on the ground, too, exactly where Abby and Chelsea had been standing seconds ago.

"Are you hurt?" Ruby asked the heap of people.

Like hands on a clock, they'd landed pointing in slightly different directions. Abby was faceup on top, legs spread-eagled, her right hand caught under Chelsea, who was facedown sandwiched between the other two. Reed was on the bottom.

"Are you guys okay?" somebody else called.

Ren Colby had come up beside Ruby. In fact, she noticed that a small crowd had gathered.

Miraculously, all three of her friends were unhurt.

Abby's bosom was heaving and Chelsea's skirt was hiked up to her hips, presenting the onlookers with a memorable view. The two of them managed to scoot off Reed and onto the ground. Sitting up, they straightened their clothes, shook out their fingers and rotated their shoulders. Apparently finding everything in working order, they took the hands the men gathering around them extended and stood up.

Reed found his feet on his own. The last one up, he brushed the dirt off his palms and then from the seat of his pants. Ruby swore Abby looked as if she wanted to help.

"You saved my life," the petite blonde said breathlessly. "There must be some way I can repay you."

"Worst-case scenario," Reed said levelly, "you would have been run over by a scooter, not a bus, Abby. You okay?"

Something bloomed inside Ruby. Glancing at Chelsea and Abby, she doubted she was the only one who appreciated his modesty almost as much as his bravery.

The owner of the bar himself cut through the little crowd that had gathered. It was unclear to Ruby if Murphy was his first name or last. In his early sixties, he was a robust man with a square face, a thick mustache and a deep booming voice. "What the hell happened?"

While Ren Colby and a few others filled him in, the boy responsible said, "The throttle stuck. I just got this scooter and I couldn't— I tried, but I guess I musta panicked. I didn't mean for— My dad's gonna kill me."

It was Reed who went to him. Ruby watched as he helped him stand the scooter up and ran his hand over the dented fender and broken spokes on the front wheel. With his bobbling Adam's apple and shaggy hair, the boy reminded her of one of the younger Jonas Brothers. She couldn't hear what Reed said, but it must have been the right thing because the teenager got his phone out of his pocket and made a call.

"Everyone here okay?" Murphy asked.

Reed scooped the crushed pizza box off the ground where they'd all landed and opened the lid. "The biggest casualty is my pizza."

"We'll get you another," Murphy exclaimed, slapping Reed on the back hard enough to cause him to wince. "On the house." He turned to Abby and Chelsea next. "You two gonna sue me?"

"For a bad pizza?" Abby quipped. "Like it's the first time that's happened."

"How're your mom and dad, Abigail?" Murphy said. "How about yours, Chelsea? Reed, you need anything besides another pizza?"

With that, the crowd began to sift back to their tables inside and out. And Ruby thought she was going to like being a part of this town.

Abby and Chelsea continued to the restrooms as they'd initially intended. Ruby stayed outside and took everything in. She noticed that Ren Colby was trying his luck with someone who'd just arrived, and the biker in the red bandanna was leaving with a hardy-looking gal wearing combat boots and a leather vest similar to his. The couple making out earlier hadn't even come up for air.

Ruby wasn't certain why she looked at Reed last. Maybe she'd felt him staring back at her. It occurred to her that she'd been wrong.

Lightning could strike tonight.

* * *

Reed felt a burning inside.

His shoulder was going to be sore as the devil tomorrow, but it wasn't that. Stepping over the rope lying on the ground, he walked directly to Ruby.

His first instinct was to move in close so she would feel the heat emanating from him and he would feel the sultriness swirling around her. He fought it, though. Resisted.

"Do you have a minute?" he asked.

He didn't catch her answer, but she led the way to a table where a leather bag hung from the back of a chair. A Prince song was playing, and a car idled at the light on the corner, its window down, the radio so loud Reed felt the bass anyplace his skin was exposed to the air. People were talking at the tables he passed. He barely heard, his eyes practically glued to Ruby. It had less to do with the fact that the fit of her jeans should be outlawed and everything to do with the fact that he was glad it wasn't.

They'd barely gotten settled in their chairs before Abby and Chelsea joined them. Close friends of his sister's, they asked about Joey and Marsh and Noah and Lacey, and relayed their daily interactions with Madeline via every social media network known to modern man. They talked and joked and laughed the way they had a hundred times before, seemingly oblivious to the tension coiling tighter inside Reed with every passing minute.

Finally they talked about leaving. Something about some story Abby was covering and a wedding Chelsea was working tomorrow. Instead of going with them, Ruby told them she'd call them in the morning. As they walked across the street and disappeared into the alley beside Bell's, the tension in Reed began to uncoil.

Ruby darted him a look after they'd gone. "You really are one of the good guys, aren't you?"

He didn't know if she was referring to his leap over that rope earlier or something else. And he didn't ask. It was beside the point.

Her skin was creamy, her cheeks touched with pink, her lips shiny. The old-fashioned gaslights in the courtyard threw shadows through her eyelashes every time she blinked and deepened the green of her top and the chestnut color of her hair, but it was her eyes—those green, green eyes—he focused on. "I hadn't planned to get into this tonight."

"Into what?" she asked plaintively.

He propped both elbows on the table and said, "A little while ago Marsh reminded me of everything riding on my actions, and my *re*actions. More precisely, on my reaction to being within twenty yards of you."

Cupping her chin thoughtfully in one hand, she said, "What *is* riding on your actions or your reactions? Are you talking about Joey?"

That she'd homed in on the heart of the issue gave him pause. The scratchy song waffling from the speakers ended. Without it, the night was quieter, almost still. He lowered his voice accordingly. "We have another appointment with the judge first thing Monday morning. He's usually fair, but he's an ornery old cuss and has the power to force us to put Joey in foster care. I can't let that happen."

"Reed?" she interrupted.

"Yes?"

"You want Joey to be yours, don't you?"

SANDRA STEFFEN

"I don't see the relevance in—"

But she interrupted him. "Why?"

"What do you mean why?" he asked.

He'd been told the sharpness in his voice could be off-putting. It didn't deter her in the least.

"A lot of guys would be secretly hoping to be let off the hook. Most guys I know would be terrified to find themselves the single parent of a baby."

"If I told you I'm not like most guys, it would sound like a line."

She looked at him without blinking. "Try giving me a straight answer," she said point-blank. "All I'm asking is why? Why does he mean so much to you? Why do you want him to be yours?"

"If I took the time to analyze *that,* I would have to take the time to analyze why I'm glad you were out with Chelsea and Abby tonight."

Her chin came up as if she'd caught something between the eyes. "Oh," she said. And then, "O-o-o-h."

She took a sip of her watered-down drink, and he took a moment to consider the best way to explain. "I assured my brother that you and I have talked about this, and are in complete agreement that neither of us has any intention of pursuing, er, anything."

"Because you're looking for a needle in a haystack and I'm not looking at all."

"Yes," he said, although he couldn't seem to stop looking. "Ruby?"

She put her glass down. Waited.

"Resisting this isn't working."

"But of course it is," she argued.

"When I just now saw you looking at me from the other side of that downed rope, I wouldn't have remembered my name if someone had asked. I don't remember how I got from there to here. That zing overruled my resistance. Marsh brought the reason to my attention earlier. What we resist persists."

She sat up a little straighter, her eyes on his. "I wouldn't have pegged your brother as a philosopher, but I'm listening."

Absently rubbing his right shoulder, Reed said, "You probably noticed we seem to keep running into each other. You've been in Orchard Hill a matter of days. How many times have we found ourselves in the same place at the same time? What does tonight make? Four times? Five?"

"Five, but—"

"So you're counting, too. Ruby, would you just stop and consider this? What if Marsh has a point? What if it's true?"

"Okay," she said a little too quickly. "For argument's sake, let's say there's something to your brother's assessment, and it's possible that the more we resist, the more this—" she motioned from her to him and back again "—persists. What do you suggest we do about it?"

"We disarm and disable the attraction," he said.

"How?"

"We stop resisting." He caught her looking at his mouth. And then she leaned down and did something to her foot under the table.

"Of course," she sputtered. "That sounds easy enough. Why didn't you say so? But how, pray tell, do you propose we do that?"

Because he couldn't help noticing how full her lower lip looked when she was being sarcastic, he said, "We delve directly past kissing. All the way."

She opened her mouth to speak, closed it and tried again. "All the way?"

"Allow me to rephrase." Leaning closer so no one around them would hear, he said, "How often do we go out with somebody only to wind up just friends in the end? A woman who looks as good as you do knows the drill. You meet someone, go out, take it to the next level and maybe you take it slow or maybe it's one fell swoop. Either way, eventually you start to notice tiny annoyances. Pretty soon they're big red flags."

She shrugged, nodded, silently agreeing he had a point.

And he continued, "What if you and I skip dating, skip the frenzy, skip the marathon and go directly to the finish line?"

Ruby found herself holding her breath. Okay, enough.

Gongs were going off inside her skull. She had to stop for a sec. She had to think. Breathing would be good. Slipping her shoe off, she absently rubbed her right big toe on her left calf and thought about the road to relationships Reed was describing.

"What exactly constitutes the finish line for you?" she asked.

He groaned quietly. "Contrary to how that sounded, I'm talking about friendship."

Oh. Well. Huh.

Leaning back in her chair, she thought about the frenzy of a new romance, the buildup and the expectations and the elation, the strategizing and all the energy expended for something that ultimately fizzled out or went sour. Reed had made a strong argument for the pro side of the just-friends debate. On the one hand it sounded absurd. Absurdity aside, she believed in the pull of the moon and the power of Venus in retrograde. She believed destiny was the mapmaker but it was the choices people made that determined their path. She also believed that sometimes there was a moment, just one moment, that changed everything. Reed had a word for that moment. *Zing.*

Something else he'd said had struck a chord in her. He'd admitted that he didn't remember walking over to her. She'd experienced a similar sensation when she'd first seen him tonight. It was as if someone had pushed the mute button on the big picture. Sound ceased and everyone in the courtyard at Murphy's disappeared.

Except him.

He was right about something else, too. They *did* keep running into one another, and each time the connection *was* stronger. Could it be that resisting only intensified the magnetic pull?

"I expected you to have more to say," he pointed out.

"Do you really believe we can be friends?" she asked.

"I don't see how we can help being friends, Ruby."

"Are you proposing that we stop resisting and go directly to BFFs?"

He shook his head the way men did when dealing with certain types of women, maybe all types of women, and then said, "A person can never have too many friends, right?"

An argument broke out at a nearby table and a waitress counting the minutes until her shift was over delivered Reed's pizza. While she trudged on over to investigate the ruckus, Reed asked, "Do you have any thoughts or questions about anything, Ruby?"

She spent a moment in quiet deliberation. "Actually, I do have one."

"Fire away."

"Did you really French-kiss Abby's sister?"

He didn't even try to hide his surprise. His golden eyebrows shot up and his storm-cloud eyes widened. "Abby told you about that?"

"She said you choirboys are the ones we have to watch out for."

"That right? I was never in the choir."

Reed Sullivan had classic bone structure and a mouth made for rakish grins. He accepted the responsibility of caring for an abandoned baby and he saved people from speeding freight trains, or scooters, whatever the case may be. If he said he'd never been a choirboy, she believed him.

"You were saying about Abby's sister," she prodded.

"Bailey and I were doing homework and had no idea her bratty kid sister was hiding in the closet. I'd made my move before I heard Abby snicker. She extorted money from both Bailey and me and promised it would be our little secret. Then Abby demonstrated what she'd seen in front of her class during show-and-tell the very next day. It was the only time I was ever called to the principal's office."

"How old were you?" she asked.

"I don't know. Fifth or sixth grade, I guess."

"That old?" she said as an Elton John song began to play.

"I was a late bloomer." His smile started in his eyes, spreading pleasantly across the rest of his face.

He was a wise guy, she thought, a tall polished wise guy with a dash of heroism and a vein of the uncivi-

lized running through him. Scooting her chair back
when he did, they both got up.

"What exactly do you do with your friends who happen to be women?" she asked. "My turn to rephrase.
What constitutes friendship in your book? I guess I'm
a little fuzzy on the next step."

"It can be whatever you want. Do you need fifty
bucks until payday? Someone to let your dog out? Do
you have any furniture that needs moving or help with
heavy lifting in general?"

She raised her right arm and made a muscle. "Have
you seen these guns? I don't have a dog and I still have
the first dollar I ever earned."

"You can't think of anything you need help with?"
He was serious.

"Not off the top of my head. I guess I'll have to
think about it and let you know."

She looked up slightly. He looked down slightly.
And they both smiled.

"Friends," he said.

"Friends," she agreed.

They shook on it, a handshake between friends.
Then they parted company, Reed with his fresh hot
pizza in his right hand and Ruby with her oversize bag
on her shoulder. Neither of them mentioned the vibration they couldn't quite brush away.

Sawing. Drilling. Pounding. Crashing.

It was Monday, and the renovations at the tavern
were well under way. The drop ceiling was lying in
hundreds, if not thousands, of pieces on the floor. A
carpenter in a tool belt was manning a vicious-looking
saw, and two others were swinging hammers. More

clanking and banging was coming from the restrooms, where the plumber was working on leaky pipes.

Ruby stood in the midst of it all, looking up at the dust sifting down from the rafters. The two guys on the ladders were responsible for the demolition. The tall one in charge looked down at her from his perch. "You need to put a hard hat on if you're going to stay. There's an extra one in the back of the truck. And watch out for upturned boards with nails sticking out."

In other words, she needed to get out of the way.

The electrician would come as soon as the demo work was complete, tomorrow most likely. And then the carpenters would return and the painters would work their magic. Finally the floors would be refinished. If everything went according to plan, the upgrades would run like clockwork.

Ruby's phone made the sound it always made when a text came in. Fishing it out of her back pocket, she carefully stepped around the debris without running a nail through the sole of her tennis shoes, which would have meant a trip to the emergency room and probably a tetanus shot, too, and strolled to the hallway leading to the restrooms.

It was from Amanda. And like the twenty-five previous texts from Ruby's best friend back home, it ended with C U @ the reunion.

They'd been at this for days. The first time, Ruby had replied, I'm coming down with a cold. Probably pneumonia. Or a tumor.

I'll be sure and pick up some vitamin C U @ the reunion.

Another time she'd typed, What's that? Reception's bad here.

Error. Excuse only valid on actual calls. C U @ the reunion.

Around the fifteenth text, Ruby had typed, You kids have fun.

We're going to. C U @ the reunion. PS Found a date yet?

Ten minutes ago, Ruby had texted, Are you a stalker? Do I know you?

Wondering what witticism Amanda would send next, Ruby veered around a pile of lumber in the hallway. A loud clank and mild swearing carried through the open door of one of the restrooms.

She read the latest text from Amanda as she went. Luv U. C U @ the reunion.

Ruby typed, Now you're playing dirty.

It's why you luv me, 2. C U @ the reunion.

Ruby did love her BFF. She'd always been lucky in the friend department. Her old friends in Gale had been supportive through the whole Cheater Peter debacle. Ruby didn't take infidelity lightly. She didn't take friendship lightly, either. She and her college roommate did a destination get-together once a year; she kept in touch with her friends in L.A., too. The new friends she'd made in Orchard Hill were turning out to be the kind with lasting-friendship potential, as well.

On Facebook, she'd *liked* the story Abby covered about ghost sightings at a local inn. And while she'd been waiting for Chelsea at the restaurant yesterday, Ruby had sent Reed the picture she snapped of the bulletin board where a note from a licensed day-care provider had been tacked. She'd seen him driving by a few hours before and returned his friendly wave.

Friends, she thought. A girl really couldn't have too many of them.

She reached the end of the hallway and noticed that the doors of the restrooms had been propped open. The bathrooms here had cracked tile floors and rust-stained sinks and corroded faucets. Those were their good features. The lights were on in both poorly lit spaces, but the clanking was coming from the ladies' room. She strode to the doorway with the intention of checking the plumber's progress, only to spin around.

It was too late. The image had been lasered onto the insides of her eyelids. Rubbing them didn't blur the picture she now carried of said plumber's, er, well, there was no pretty word for that part of an overweight man's anatomy.

Criminy. Humans had the capability to send messages around the world at the speed of light via computers that fit in the palms of their hands. And yet no one had been successful in designing a belt that could hold up a plumber's jeans.

She was still grimacing when her phone chirruped. It wasn't a text this time but an actual call.

It was Reed.

"Quick," she said, stepping into the alley outside. "Say something to erase what I just mistakenly witnessed in the ladies' room here at Bell's."

"I thought you had an eidetic memory," he said.

"I didn't say your job was going to be easy."

He laughed, but it sounded tense.

"I hear Joey crying," she said, squinting in the sudden brightness outdoors. "That's good, right? It's not good that he's crying, but the fact that he's crying at your place means your meeting with the judge went well." When Reed said nothing, she added, "Did it go well?"

"We've been granted another week's reprieve. So far the judge hasn't decided Joey would be better off in foster care than with Marsh and me. When it comes to deciding what's best for minor children, the court system is holding all the cards."

Ruby had heard horror stories about small children being literally ripped out of their parents' arms by a well-meaning social worker. No wonder he and Marsh were worried.

He must have picked Joey up because now it sounded as if the baby was crying directly in Ruby's ear. "It's one o'clock," she said, wondering how Reed could possibly hear her, or anything else, for that matter. "I thought you and Marsh were interviewing a potential nanny at one."

"Marsh went to Tennessee with Sam. The woman from the agency isn't here yet. Tardiness. Strike one."

"What's wrong with Joey?" she asked.

"What? Hold on." He must have moved his phone to his other ear. "What did you say?"

"I was just wondering why Joey's crying." *Her* ear was ringing. She could only imagine what all that wailing was doing to Reed's.

"Good question. He ate. He burped. He isn't wet.

He does this sometimes. Not often, thank God. Wait. I think someone drove in."

The crying continued. Gosh, the kid sure had a set of lungs.

"False alarm," Reed said. "No one's here."

Ruby imagined Reed walking the baby from room to room, jiggling him, patting him, doing everything he could to soothe him. "Have you tried singing to him?" she asked.

"What do you think started all this?"

She smiled, and imagined him smiling, too. "Did you call for any particular reason?" she asked.

"I'm killing time. I wondered if you've thought of anything you'd like help with."

"Not yet," she answered.

The *waaa-waaa-waaaaing* continued. "The woman you're interviewing still isn't there?"

"No."

"How long will Joey keep this up?"

"I'll have to ask him."

Men, she thought. But this time she was sure she'd heard a smile in his voice. "Let me know what he says, okay?"

"I'll do that."

Joking aside, Reed and Marsh desperately needed to hire someone to help with Joey's care, and in order to do that they needed to make a good impression. "You know, Reed," she said, filling a plastic can with the hose and watering the parched petunias in the barrel at the bottom of her stairs. "It might be divine providence that that woman's late. If Joey is screaming like a banshee when she drives up, she might run the other way."

"I feel better, thanks."

Laughing, she set the empty watering can inside the door and looked at the dust settling on the ladder leaning up against the wall and the lumber stacked underneath it. Reed and Marsh needed the help of professionals as much as she did. Feeling in the way here, she had an idea.

"Reed?"

Silence. Well, not total silence. Joey was still screaming.

"Reed? Can you hear me?"

But his attention was on Joey. "It's okay, buddy. I've got you. Don't worry. Everything's going to be all right."

Something went soft inside her and she heard herself say, "I'll be right there."

Chapter Seven

Ruby lifted Joey a little higher against her chest and tried not to grimace. Those muscles she'd bragged about Friday night were getting quite a workout and her trainer weighed less than thirteen pounds. She might never be able to straighten her elbow again, but it was a small price to pay.

Checking their reflection in the mirror outside Reed's den, she saw that Joey's eyes were only half open and his cheek was scrunched where it lay against her shoulder. His little bow lips were puckered and a dark spot was forming on her shirt beneath them. He was almost asleep. Mission nearly accomplished.

She padded quietly from room to room in the sprawling hundred-year-old house, listening to the clear concise tones of Reed's voice. He was in the process of conducting another interview in the kitchen.

Good grief, she thought, halfway around the dining room table. Had he really just asked Nanny McPhee's double if she'd ever been spanked?

Ruby had arrived three minutes ahead of the first interviewee. Operating under the assumption that Ruby had never seen a baby, let alone held one, Reed had asked a gazillion questions about her capabilities. She supposed she shouldn't have been surprised that being his *friend* didn't exempt her from careful scrutiny where Joey was concerned. She'd been only too happy to put his mind at ease, but all right already. Time was a-wasting.

"Reed," she'd insisted loud enough to be heard over the baby's earsplitting wails. "I bought my first car with babysitting money. It was this sweet cobalt-blue SHO—well, it had one green door and an orange fender, but everything else was blue. Do you know how many babysitting jobs it takes to save enough money to buy a car?"

Seeing his eyes narrow speculatively, she'd added, "That was rhetorical. Suffice it to say I was in great demand. I love babies. I love politicians who love babies. Some of my best friends used to be babies. I'm good with them. They like me. They do."

Joey had cried on.

Gesturing to his little head and then to his equally little bottom, she'd said, "This is the end you feed and this is the end you diaper. See? I'm practically an expert."

She'd held out her hands in silent expectation. And still Reed had been reluctant to hand him over.

"I'll guard him with my life. I promise."

Magic words, evidently. The doorbell had rung

while Reed was transferring the fitful baby to her arms. By the time she'd completed her second circuit through the sprawling house with its decidedly masculine furnishings, Joey's cries had lost their vehemence and the interview for a nanny had begun.

The first candidate of the day had been youngish and slender and not very tall. Wearing navy slacks and a white blouse befitting nannyhood, she had been as perky as Mary Poppins herself. While Ruby had walked and swayed and softly patted Joey, the young woman had recited an impressive work history for someone her age.

Apparently the baby knew something Ruby didn't. He grabbed a fistful of her hair and, still fussing, settled in for the ride.

Reed had seemed impressed with the young woman's credentials, too. In fact, he'd sounded very friendly in the interview, warm and understanding and cordial, as if he was going to be a wonderful boss. Things were going *super,* which apparently was Nanny Number One's favorite word.

A few questions about where she'd received her education led to more about where she liked to hang out and who she hung with, her favorite movies and her favorite sports team. The personal questions had turned out to be her downfall, for she developed collywobbles of the mouth, and soon she was telling Reed about her mother and soon-to-be ex-stepfather and how her boyfriend wanted to move in with her but she just wasn't sure because she might get a dog instead, and besides he was allergic.

Ruby closed her eyes on the young woman's behalf. Oh, boy. Too much information.

By the time the next woman had arrived, Joey was doing that little hiccuppy thing babies did when their crying jag was over but the memory of it remained. Notoriously too nosy for her own good, Ruby had peeked out the window and watched as a heavyset woman ambled up the sidewalk. Looking very much like a headmistress or perhaps a monk, she had short frizzing gray hair and a square face and wore a loose-fitting gunmetal-gray sack dress.

She'd told Reed she'd worked for the same family for fifteen years and was looking for another good fit. The spanking question had given the woman pause. Ruby imagined Reed must have been smiling benignly at her from across the kitchen table, because the grandmother of two confided that "her mama had done a little spanking in her day."

"Obviously she raised you to be a woman of strong character," Reed said.

"Why, thank you. It's so nice to discover somebody your age on the same page in that department. The apple doesn't fall far from the tree, believe you me. It's like I tell my daughter. Sometimes a little swat placed just so really gets their attention, doesn't it?"

Ruby could hardly believe her ears. Who knew collywobbles of the mouth was viral?

Reed was good, she thought. Sneaky good. If she hadn't been holding the baby, she would have taken notes. Wondering if he'd learned those tactics in Basic Interviewing 101 or if he'd developed the skills on his own, she made a mental note to remember them tomorrow when she met with one of the applicants for the bartending position at Bell's.

It wasn't long before Joey was humming in his sleep

and Reed was seeing the second woman to the door. Joey remained nannyless. No surprises there.

Reed stared out the window over the sink as the abrasive old bat flounced out the door. Squeezing the bridge of his nose, he closed his eyes. Joey's last crying jag had left his right ear ringing and that second interview had left a bad taste in his mouth.

Both women had been highly recommended by the agency, and he'd had high hopes that one of them would live up to her reputation. He could have overlooked the older one's chin hairs and even the grating sound of her voice, but her philosophy on discipline was not acceptable to him and it wouldn't be to Marsh, either.

The first interview had gone better. He'd been willing to give her a chance despite her tardiness. A flat tire was a plausible, understandable excuse. The fact that she'd handled it and hadn't canceled the interview was even commendable. He could have excused her drama-queen prattle, too. If only she hadn't failed the most important criterion of all. She hadn't asked to meet Joey.

He couldn't allow someone so disinterested to care for his—for Joey. He wouldn't.

The pad of footsteps sounded behind him. "Are Mary Poppins and Nanny McPhee both gone?" Ruby asked.

He let out a breath and turned around.

Ruby had arrived an hour ago in the nick of time in faded jeans, a Red Wings T-shirt and tennis shoes. Her curly hair was even more mussed now, her head tipped a bit to the left. Joey was sound asleep at her shoulder, his favorite position in the world.

Missing a sock again, the baby didn't look as if he had a care in the world. Now, why on earth did Reed suddenly feel as if an invisible fist had him by the vocal cords? He cleared his throat, swallowed. "You really do know a thing or two about babies," he finally said.

"Told you."

She did this little thing with her nose, wrinkling it slightly in a show of pained tolerance. It shouldn't have sent an electrical current through him.

He was becoming accustomed to Ruby's Florence Nightingale generosity, her uncommon kindness and good nature. She probably offered the same open helpfulness to all her friends.

Friends.

Cliché or not, friendship really was the means and the solution here. Win-win. His own words replayed through his mind. *Skip the frenzy, skip the marathon and go directly to the finish line.* Running metaphors, he thought. Not his most profound work, but it was the best he'd been able to come up with on the fly.

Crossing the room in four long strides, he said, "Here, I'll take him before your arm goes completely numb. It's amazing how heavy he can get when he's asleep."

Transferring a sleeping baby was never smooth. In this instance, it resulted in a yelp from Ruby. "Wait," she said. "He's tangled in my hair."

They stopped halfway through the switch, four hands holding one small baby. Joey's head was turned in his sleep, his arm extended, his fingers squeezed tight around a thick lock of curly hair.

"Sure," she said quietly, "*now* he's out like a light. Do you think you could get him to loosen the stranglehold he has on my hair or should we just yank that section out?"

Reed found himself smiling. Carefully shifting Joey back to her, he went to work untangling chestnut strands of spun silk from one unbelievably small and strong fist.

He and Ruby stood close together, her slender hand resting along Joey's back, her head tipped slightly in order to give Reed better access to the hair spilling over her shoulder. It was almost a relief when she started talking.

"My brother's little girl used to get her hands tangled up in her own hair. The more upset she got, the more she pulled, and the harder she pulled, the more she cried," she said.

"You have brothers, too?" He worked as quickly as possible, focused on the task.

"Just one. Rusty, well, his name is Connor but everyone calls him Rusty. He's my twin brother, actually. We're not identical."

He laughed because obviously a brother and sister could not be identical. "One unidentical twin brother and one niece? How old is she?"

"Kamryn is five. For an entire year we all believed she was Rusty's baby. No one knew the truth except his fiancée, who turned out to be a slut in disguise. His ex-fiancée now. I'm not sure if she's still a slut, but she probably is. We all really miss her. Kamryn, not the heartless ex."

Reed's fingers stilled for a moment, his gaze going to hers. She looked back at him, her eyes wide and green and guileless as she said, "Collywobbles of the mouth *is* contagious. I knew it."

He laughed. And he swore the house sighed. Perhaps that was his vocal cords unfurling. Ruby's affability, her easygoing outgoing loquaciousness was almost contagious, too.

Almost.

"It's nice that you don't hold grudges," he said.

"That's what I always say."

"So no husband or kids of your own yet?" he asked.

She tapped her foot. "No kids, no husband, not even an ex-husband. I know, right? I'll be thirty in a little over a year. I was almost engaged once, but alas, we were too young. I told him we needed to finish high school, or at the very least the ninth grade. Now he's a priest. Tell me he didn't take the breakup hard. I mean, seriously, a commitment to a lifetime of celibacy speaks for itself, don't you think?"

Reed didn't know when he'd met a woman with a drier sense of humor, but decided it might be best to bypass any discussions about celibacy for the time being. "There, you're untangled." He took Joey back into his arms, tucked Joey's arm to his side and smoothed the hair he'd just freed off Ruby's shoulder away from the sleeping child.

His fingers stilled. He hadn't meant the contact to be anything more than…anything, really. And yet it felt like…something. She must have felt it, too, for her eyes darted to his and just as quickly away.

They both recovered with about as much subtlety as the refrigerator clanking on. Taking a giant step backward, she gingerly rubbed her scalp and said, "I told Marty, Father Marty now, that if he happens to reconsider the whole priesthood thingy before I leave my childbearing years completely behind, we can still have our little Madison and Montana. Probably not the best thing to tell a man at his ordainment."

Reed laughed again. The momentary awkwardness between them gone, he said, "You're something else, you know that?"

"That's what all my friends say." He noticed she was smiling, too.

Her phone made the same sound his made when a text was coming in. She disappeared into the next room for a moment and came back with her phone and her keys.

"Did you think of anything yet?" he asked, his arms tightening around Joey.

Absently checking her message, she said, "Have I thought of anything about what?"

"Have you thought of anything I can do to help *you* for a change?"

"Oh, that. Not yet," she answered on her way to the door. "I need to get back to Bell's. Work on the renovations has begun. If you're in the neighborhood in the next couple of days, stop by."

"I'll do that," he said. He walked her to the door, held it with his free hand. "Thanks again, Ruby."

She did that thing with her nose once more. "That's what friends are for, pal."

He watched her go, and saw her dash off a text on her way to her car. The last thing he heard through the screen before she got in her vehicle was her rich, luscious, sultry laugh.

Ruby reread Amanda's latest text while she put her seat belt on. Ran into Jason. Asked about you. Bet he'd be your date for the reunion. C U @ said event.

Jason Horning had had a crush on Ruby since kindergarten. She'd been a head taller than him then, too.

I'd rather go with Father Marty, she typed back.

Not acceptable. I'll think of something. C U @ the reunion.

Can't talk, Ruby typed. Trapped under something heavy.

She'd barely started her car before the next text arrived. a. Person b. Place c. Animal or d. Thing? If it's a. spare no details. C U @ the reunion.

Ruby shook her head and backed around Reed's Mustang. Her best friend in Gale had a one-track mind. It was only one of the reasons they got along so well.

Friends, she thought, adjusting her rearview mirror— now, why on earth did she turn it so she could see her own eyes?

She'd called Reed pal.

Pal. Buddy. Comrade. Chum. Amigo. Bro. All were synonyms for friend, which was what he was, what she was, what they were. Friends.

She checked for traffic and pulled onto the paved road. Friendship was…peaceful. It may not have been as invigorating as *the frenzy,* but it was nice, pleasant, enjoyable, even. Safe. Being friends beat resisting, hands down.

She neared the four-way stop on the corner of Old Orchard Highway and Orchard Road, both named by early Dutch settlers who reputedly squandered nothing, not when naming roads and city streets or even their children, for that matter, who quietly and unobtrusively went their entire lives without middle names. An old woman eating by herself at the Hill had shared that particular gem of folklore only yesterday. Ruby enjoyed hearing about legendary people and myths and memories. She always had. She had one of those faces people talked to, she thought as she coasted to a halt at the corner. It was a good barkeeper's face.

A friendly face. Waiting her turn, she glanced in the mirror—nobody was behind her—and met her own gaze once again. Choosing the friendship route with Reed was turning out to be exactly what they both seemed to need. A few minutes ago she'd been standing statue-still a foot away from him, his breath warm on her cheek and his fingers gentle in her hair. Her toe had been on its best behavior.

Friendship definitely cured the zing. Her hand went to the tendrils he'd touched. Well, for the most part, anyway.

Two days later, Ruby stood in the middle of her tavern and viewed the renovation's progress, although lack of progress would be a more fitting description. Work had come to a screeching halt yesterday—some problem with the authenticity of a temporary permit, which had turned out to be a perfectly legitimate piece of paper. By the time she'd gotten that verified in writing from the correct city servant *twenty-six* hours later, the drywall hangers had started their next remodel and wouldn't be able to squeeze Bell's back into their schedule until Friday, *at the earliest*.

Ruby had many fine qualities. This she knew for a fact. She was kind, helpful, nonjudgmental, socially tolerant, accepting and generally quite friendly, not to mention a lot of fun.

Patient, she wasn't.

She stomped around the cavernous room where the jukebox and tables and chairs had been. The billiards tables were covered with tarps, as were the old, ornately carved bar and all seven attached stools, which was good. Once the renovations were completed and the protective plastic was removed, a little tung oil and elbow grease would bring out the bar's best features, mars, scratches, scars and all. The plumber had finished his work in both restrooms. Again, that was a good thing. The mountain of broken pieces of the yellowed, disgusting drop ceiling had been shoveled into buckets and carried out to a rented Dumpster. The positives were adding up.

Friday at the earliest? Were they kidding?

All right, she told herself, her hands in her back pockets, the curls around her face springing free of the knot high on the back of her head. This wasn't the end of the world. As long as the drywall crew returned when they said they would, Bell's would still be ready to open on time. It wasn't best-case scenario, but it was doable, and doable was fine.

Fine wasn't elation, but, she decided as she turned out the lights and locked the door, there was nothing she could do about it. Friday at the earliest.

Oh, brother.

Wandering around her new apartment hours later, she was still clenching. She'd gone over the beer, wine and liquor order with a fine-tooth comb and would place it first thing in the morning. She'd come across an advertisement online for a restaurant liquidation sale, and chose her top-ten favorite one-of-a-kind drink titles. She even began designing the simple menu. She'd invited Abby and Chelsea to see a movie playing at the newly reopened theater downtown. But Chelsea was in Grand Rapids at a bridal show and Abby was meeting somebody she met online. Ruby hadn't felt like going alone.

Her mother had called, and her brother and Amanda, too. Even though she didn't ask for their opinions, her mom said she was PMSing and Amanda said "this too shall pass" and her brother suggested she should either get drunk or laid or both.

She should have known better than to complain. Hormones, idioms, booze and sex. They'd certainly covered everything. Unfortunately, it didn't make her feel any less like chewing glass.

Finally, she'd taken a shower and changed into yoga pants and a tank top she'd washed so many times it was as soft as a second skin. Feeling refreshed and comfortable, if not happy-snappy, she thought about grabbing a bite to eat and considered going to bed without it. She looked at her phone. Gosh, it was only nine o'clock. Seriously?

For lack of a better idea, she wandered onto the stoop for a little fresh air. Though shadowy here in the alley, it *was* still broad daylight. Was she stuck in a time warp?

Interestingly, a silver Mustang was pulling to a stop down below. Reed got out and looked up at her, his feet apart, brown chinos slightly wrinkled, the sleeves of his white shirt rolled halfway up his forearms.

She waited until the clock on the courthouse completed its ninth chime to say, "That's two minutes slow."

"Has been for years," he called up. "Elementary-school teachers have incorporated it into basic math lessons. If the courthouse clock is two minutes slow and the clock strikes seven, what time will it be in fifteen minutes?"

Another interesting tidbit of area folklore, she thought. "What are you doing here?"

"I'm taking you up on your invitation to show me the renovations at Bell's."

"They're at a standstill until Friday at the earliest." She couldn't control her little sneer. "I was just thinking I missed dinner. You're welcome to join me."

"Do you cook?"

"Not well."

"What are you having?" Obviously he was picking up on her less than jovial mood.

"Triple fudge ice cream. It's called Death by Chocolate, which has to be better than Death by Friday at the Earliest."

She could see him trying not to grin as he started up the stairs. Leaving him to find his own way in, she headed to the kitchen for the bowls and spoons.

Reed took the steps two at a time and strolled through the door Ruby had left open. The last time he'd been here, music had been playing and the room had been in wild disarray. Tonight her small apartment was quiet, the sectional in its rightful place opposite the TV, the rug rolled out flat. There was a large conch shell on the trunk she was using as a coffee table and a green-and-blue watercolor on one wall.

Ruby was drying her hands when he entered the minuscule kitchen. "Rough day?" he asked, eyeing the tub of Death by Chocolate ice cream.

She answered without looking up from the carton she was opening. "More like a missed window of opportunity." She paused, as if pondering something. With a mild shake of her head, she reached for a bright yellow ice-cream scoop and got busy.

The antiquated fluorescent lights overhead flickered the way old fluorescent lights often did, and every ten seconds the oscillating fan on the table stirred the air in their direction. Ruby wore knit pants and a faded tank top that had been washed so thin the lace of her bra showed through. Beneath that lace, her breasts rose and fell with her every breath. Concentrating on her task, she spooned ice cream into the first of two flowered bowls. One scoop, two.

"Strawberry jam or grape?" he asked hurriedly, forcing his gaze elsewhere.

"Strawberry jam or grape what?" she grumbled, adding another scoop.

"It's a getting-to-know-you question." It happened to be more than that, a lot more, for with it he was trying to distract his wayward thoughts and the way he was reacting to Ruby.

Seeing her skewing her mouth to one side in serious contemplation, he said, "There's no right or wrong answer." When it became apparent she wasn't going to reply, he studied her expression even more closely. "Okay, let's try another one. You were listening to vintage music when I stopped by to get Lacey's cameras the other day. Which do you prefer, Guns N' Roses or Leonard Cohen?"

"That's another tough one," she said.

He eyed the bowl that was getting so full he didn't see how it could hold any more. She found room, though.

"Give it a whirl," he said. "Choose one."

Pulling a face, she set an open jar of fudge topping in the microwave and started filling the second bowl. "Music is one of the reasons I bought a bar," she finally said. "Did I tell you I want to have live music on Saturday nights? And that old jukebox in the back still works, a bonus if there ever was one. Music is kind of my thing. You name it, I like it—rap, country, heavy metal, classical, anything old most of all. Billy Joel, ACDC, the Rolling Stones, Elvis, Waylan Jennings, Mozart, the Pointer Sisters."

"Fair enough," he said. "What's your favorite color?"

Noticing her inner struggle again, he was beginning to see a pattern. "Cats or dogs?" he asked.

Silence.

"Sunrise or sunset?"

Sticking a spoon into the mound of ice cream, she held the bowl out to him.

"Trains or airplanes?" He took a step closer.

She crossed her eyes.

"Summer or winter?" Another step brought him within reach of her.

"Did I mention I have trouble making up my mind?" she asked.

"Day or night?"

"Reed?" The fan whirred. The fluorescent lights flickered. And she raised her gaze to his.

"Yes, Ruby?"

"What are you doing?"

"That ice cream's for me, right?"

"Of course." The microwave dinged, and she said, "Would you care for some hot fudge?"

"There isn't room in my bowl," he answered.

He wasn't surprised that struck her as funny. Tipping her head back, she started to laugh. She had a marvelous laugh. He'd noticed that before. Rich and sultry, it floated out of her like the lyrics of a song, making him glad he'd stopped by.

She returned the nearly empty carton to the freezer, and added hot fudge to the chocolate concoction in her bowl. He watched her take her first bite and saw the rapture on her face. Sampling his, he was struck anew by the differences between men and women. There was only one activity that brought men that much pleasure.

"You don't have Joey with you," she said after she'd taken the edge off whatever was fueling her ice-cream marathon. "That must mean Marsh is back. How did his trip to Tennessee go?"

It was Reed's turn to shrug.

With a wrinkling of her nose, she said, "Don't expect me to answer questions if you won't."

"You didn't answer any questions." Watching her turn a spoonful of ice cream upside down in her mouth, he considered telling her about Sam's newest discovery. It was the biggest lead they'd had yet. Nothing had been verified and certainly nothing had been proven, but Sam was getting closer to finding the woman behind Joey's sudden appearance on their doorstep. Reed felt it in the pit of his stomach. Her identity still hovered slightly out of reach like a word on the tip of his tongue, as vital as the air he breathed.

For some reason, when he opened his mouth, that

wasn't what he said. "Your first car was a blue SHO with one green door. Mine was my dad's old Charger. He handed me the keys the day I accepted the scholarship from Purdue. Told me if I was going to college on my own brainpower-induced nickel, the least he could do was give me wheels to get there. He knew I had my eye on a future in some sprawling city like Houston or Seattle or maybe Miami, but for those next four years, he wanted me to have a way home.

"Every time I pulled into the driveway for a weekend at the orchard, he'd invariably lay his hand on the hood of that car and say, 'She's yours now, son. You keep her in gas and oil changes, and she'll get you where you need to go.'"

The windows in Ruby's upstairs apartment were open, but Division Street was quiet this time of the night in the middle of the week. Other than the whir of the fan and the hum of the fluorescent lighting, her kitchen had grown quiet, too. She ate her ice cream slowly, and didn't ask why he was telling her this or what his father's gift meant to him. Maybe that was why he continued.

"It was ten below zero the day I got Marsh's call. I knew by the way he said my name it was bad. Then he told me about the accident. How Mom and Dad were dead. But Noah was okay. Madeline, too."

Reed stared into the spinning blades of the fan, but it wasn't the blur of metal he saw. "The temperature was ten below zero and yet that car started the first time I turned the key. There are two hundred seventeen miles between West Lafayette and our driveway. I don't remember one thing about the drive that night, but Dad was right. The Charger he entrusted to me took me where I needed to go. It brought me home."

Surfacing, he found himself standing across the small room from Ruby. Her ankles were crossed, her lower back resting against the counter, her spoon in one hand, her empty bowl in the other. It was hotter than blazes in here, and the humidity had made her hair curlier and her skin dewy. He wondered if she knew she was naturally beautiful, gorgeous really.

Her spoon and bowl clattered as she set them in the sink near the bright yellow ice-cream scooper. Hooking her thumbs on the counter on either side of her waist, she said, "Whatever happened to that Charger?"

She didn't ask how he'd managed to draw a breath after he'd heard the news. She didn't ask how he'd made it home during the worst blizzard of the decade, or how it'd felt when he got there.

No. Not Ruby. She asked the one question he could answer.

"Noah wrapped it around a tree two years later. He and Lacey are getting back from their honeymoon this weekend. If you see him, make sure you mention how lucky he is to be alive. Not because of the wreck, although it was a miracle he survived that. He's lucky I didn't strangle him with my bare hands."

"I haven't actually met Lacey's husband yet. I'm sure that will get us off to a great start."

He nodded in total agreement.

Later, he wouldn't recall whether they'd shared a smile then. They changed the subject, and conversation ultimately turned to her plans for Bell's, the varieties of apples grown in Reed's family orchard and a new secret graft Marsh was working on. She told him about the going-out-of-business sale at a restaurant in Sparta and the barware she hoped to purchase there.

Taking his forgotten bowl from him, she said, "I take it you're not the Death by Chocolate type."

He let his gaze flick over her once more, at her wildly curly hair and her slender shoulders and the outline of lace under her shirt. "If you mean am I a girl, no."

She gave him one of her deep, sultry chuckles while he glanced at a new text buzzing in from Marsh. "My brother's wondering where I am. You'd think he hadn't eaten in a week."

She asked, "Where are you going for takeout tonight?"

"What would you recommend?" He started for the door.

"You're on your own, pal. You saw what I had for dinner."

Reed thought she hadn't been fibbing when she said she had trouble making up her mind. There was a smile in his voice as he said, "Good night, Ruby."

Ruby followed Reed as far as her stoop and watched him start down the stairs. Darkness had fallen, and the air was starting to cool. She could hear the music at Murphy's through the alley and across the street. In the opposite direction someone was calling to a dog.

"Reed?"

The dog ran by, leash flying behind him as Reed turned around. "Yes?"

"Cats," she called. "And dogs. And goldfish. And armadillos. And ponies. Not snakes, though, or mice. *Maybe* gerbils but no rats."

He was laughing when he got in his car and drove

away. She went inside and stood resting her back along the length of her door.

They were opposites, the two of them. She was chatty. He wasn't. She was wearing the most comfortable clothes in the world. He wore a white shirt with a button-down collar and flat-front chinos. She'd complained about the delay in renovations, and he'd reminded her of Bell's potential.

She'd begun the evening in a funk. And so had he. Whatever had been bothering him when he'd arrived had still been on his mind when he left, but Ruby was beginning to understand why he wanted Joey to be his. It had to do with a tragic accident that tore a hole through an entire family, and one small baby who was somehow closing the gap.

As she stood at the kitchen sink rinsing out the bowls, she thought her mother and best friend and brother had been wrong. Her irascible mood had lifted and it hadn't been a shift in hormones or some trite saying or even the art of getting drunk or laid, or both, as Rusty had so eloquently put it.

It was conversation that went nowhere and silences that went everywhere. It was talking and not talking. It was comfortable and it wasn't. It was Reed. Yawning, she stretched her hands over her head and smiled for no particular reason.

Triple-fudge ice cream hadn't hurt.

Chapter Eight

Up and down Division Street, veterans, some of whom looked too young to shave and others so old they could barely shave themselves anymore, had teamed up with members of the city council and the high school marching band to collect for the upcoming Fourth of July fireworks display. They stood in incongruous teams of four or five on nearly every corner, the city officials accepting the donations, the patriots accepting praise and gratitude, and the band members playing their hearts out.

Ruby reached into her trunk for another cardboard box, and smiled at the somewhat discordant notes of "My Country 'tis of Thee." Scattered as they were over a seven-block area, the clarinet players tended to be a few notes behind the French horns and trombones, and the drums occasionally missed the fourth beat. She couldn't see the tuba player from here, but every so often she heard "thank you" in tuba notes. She smiled every time.

Today she *was* smiling. It was Saturday, and Saturdays were always good days. The weather was especially glorious. The drywall crew had come back to Bell's yesterday, and the renovations were on track once again. Everything she would need for Bell's reopening, from beer to wine to whiskey and seltzer water, had been ordered and was due to arrive in plenty of time for the Big Day.

Abby Fitzpatrick, reporter, photographer and advertising wizard for the *Orchard Hill News* had helped Ruby design the perfect ad, which would run in the paper this coming weekend and every day thereafter until the grand reopening. Ruby was practically giddy. To top it off, her first auction had been enormously successful.

Humming along to the "Battle Hymn of the Republic" now, she hefted another box laden with her new used barware into her arms. She spun around, and almost ran headlong into the man who'd planted himself between her and Bell's front door.

She let out a little yelp. "Reed!" Before she could drop the box filled with glassware, he took it out of her hands, and not gently, either.

"Where did you come from?" Glancing around, she didn't see his car. Somebody really needed to put bells on him.

Without a word, he turned on his heel and disappeared into her tavern. Ruby spared a look at the window-shoppers in front of the shoe store down the street and wondered what on earth Reed's problem could be. Reaching all the way to the back of her trunk, she pulled another box toward her and took it inside.

She found Reed in the tavern's kitchen, where he was pacing between the antiquated grill and the extra-deep and equally old metal sink. Every surface in the small room held boxes containing her new used barware and the dozens of other items she'd picked up for a song at her first auction ever.

Reed stopped to glare at her in front of the stainless-steel exhaust fan. "You couldn't have gotten all this in your car."

That sounded like an accusation to her. "I did, actually. It's taken two trips to Sparta and back but—"

"We have a brand-new extended cab pickup sitting in the shed at the orchard," Reed cut in.

Eyeing all the cartons filled with dishes and glasses she needed to unpack and wash, and then arrange on the open shelves to the left of the sink, she bit her lip. She was starting to see where this was going.

"How many times have I given you the opportunity to ask for my help with something, with anything?" he asked.

Actually, she knew the answer, but simply said, "You have so much going on in your life."

"That's not the point."

The fit and style of Reed's clothes was worthy of *GQ,* the colors a combination of thunderclouds and smoke, like his eyes today. He'd worn a similar expression the first time she'd seen him. She didn't think failing to ask him for help was in the same category as being run off the road by some fool driving like a bat out of hell on Old Orchard Highway, but there it was, thunderclouds and smoke and a tightly clenched jaw. Suppressed anger, *GQ*-style.

"If it makes you feel any better, there are more boxes in the backseat," she said.

He obtusely failed to see the humor. She'd known men sporting similar expressions, as if pent-up steam was about to blast a hole through the tops of their heads. Her father and brother normally punctuated the display with a snort. Reed shot past her without making a sound.

He was on his way in with another armload by the time she reached the front door. "Friends ask friends for help when they need it," he said as he blew past her, glassware clanking as he went.

The volunteers were using the alley today, so after the sale she'd backed her loaded car into a parking space out front. Somebody had parked a little close on the driver's side, but the passenger side had plenty of room for her to open the door, which she did. Reed was there suddenly, reaching past her into the backseat, his shoulder brushing her arm, his hip nudging hers. Even though she backed up as far as the door would allow, there was only a matter of inches between them when he straightened.

In the tight space, she felt the heat radiating from him, and the tight coil he had on his temper. He didn't hold his pose for long. Turning on his heel, he shot past her yet again.

"Strawberry jam or grape?" she called.

He'd taken three steps before he exhaled, two more before he stopped. "Strawberry jam or grape what?" he asked, his back to her, ramrod straight, his shoulders rigid.

"It's a friendly getting-to-know-you question."

He faced her slowly, the box in his arms, a scowl on his face. "Grape."

As the marching band launched into "Home on the Range," she said, "I can see that about you. Cats or dogs?"

She could tell he was fighting a losing battle to stay angry. "If you must know, horses."

She grabbed a box of dishware, too. Falling into step beside him, she said, "Did you have horses when you were growing up?"

"A gelding named Stud."

"I'll bet he appreciated the vote of confidence." She knew she was out of hot water when one corner of Reed's mouth twitched. "Sunrise or sunset?" she asked.

Ever the gentleman, he waited for her to precede him through the door. He kept her guessing through two more trips to her car and back made in silence. After closing the trunk, he brushed the dust off his hands, and then took a pair of sunglasses from his pocket. She was in the process of swiping her hands on her gray T-shirt that covered all but the bottom few inches of her shorts when he said, "Sam has a new lead."

She stopped what she was doing and looked at him. She couldn't see his eyes through the dark lenses, but she felt him watching her. "That's good, right?"

"He has footage from a surveillance camera at a private airstrip outside Charleston. Even though the image was slightly grainy, one of the passengers bears an uncanny resemblance to the woman Marsh fell for on Roanoke Island last summer."

Shading her eyes with one hand, she asked, "Where was she going?"

"She was boarding a small private commuter plane for Detroit the same day we discovered Joey on our porch. That's some coincidence, isn't it?"

"Was there any evidence of Joey in that footage?" she asked.

He shook his head. "No baby, no diaper bag, no car seat, nothing but a small carry-on slung over her shoulder. I know. There's an enormous piece missing from the puzzle. Marsh thinks it was Julia, though."

The breeze ruffled the collar of Reed's shirt and stirred the leaves in the ornamental trees lining Division Street. She and Reed stood together in the dappled shade for a moment listening to the marching band play "Stars and Stripes Forever."

Marsh was searching high and low for a woman named Julia who may or may not have been seen boarding a plane for Detroit without a baby or any items a baby would need, and Reed was looking for a woman who may or may not have gotten pregnant as a result of a Fourth-of-July-rockets'-red-glare one-night stand. He hadn't actually used that terminology when he'd explained the situation to her, but she imagined a man like Reed would set off plenty of fireworks between a woman's sheets.

She wondered how Reed and Marsh stood so many unanswered questions. Their patience was humbling, for she'd nearly crawled out of her skin over a delay in Bell's renovations. The sooner the Sullivans received the results of the paternity test, the better.

"Sunset," he said out of the blue.

"Pardon me?" she said, not following the change in topic.

"You asked. I prefer sunset."

She glanced up at him and almost smiled at his take-it-or-leave-it attitude. "Summer or winter?"

Reed assumed his apparent favorite pose, feet apart, hands on his hips, head cocked slightly. "Fall."

"That wasn't one of the options. Have you always made your own rules?"

"Look who's talking. You could have asked for a helping hand today. I would have loaned you a pickup or gone with you, for that matter."

Slipping her hands into her back pockets, she said, "I can see that now, but it didn't occur to me at the time. If it's any consolation, I didn't ask to borrow a vehicle from Abby or Chelsea, either."

"The last I knew, Chelsea has never driven her Audi down a dirt road, and Abby's car isn't much bigger than she is. Logically, why would you have asked to borrow a ride from them?"

"We're being logical?" Ruby quipped.

"You're incorrigible," he said.

He smiled, though. And so did she.

"Heavy metal or alternative?" she asked as he started away from her down the sidewalk. When he said nothing, she called, "If you can't make up your mind, I understand. You can text me your answer. And it takes one to know one."

She couldn't quite bring herself to say pal. For some reason, that prickled the back of her mind and then stayed there.

He opened his door and got in his car, which was visible now that a panel truck had backed out of the space beside him. He didn't wave as he drove away. He smiled, though. And then he was gone.

Another hot breeze wafted through town and one

patriotic song ended and another began. Ruby remained for a moment in the dappled shade in front of Bell's. Something had shifted between her and Reed today, and she couldn't put her finger on what had changed.

She looked down, wiggled her toes. All ten of them, with their bright pink polish, sat prettily at the ends of her narrow feet, nestled in her flip-flops, not buzzing, not tingling.

The area beneath her breastbone where forgotten dreams waited, though? There was plenty happening there.

That worried her most of all.

A few days later, Ruby sat across from Chelsea and Abby in her favorite booth at the Hill. Smelling of stroganoff, fried chicken, strong coffee and strawberry-rhubarb pie, the restaurant was as crowded and noisy as it always was on Fridays at one. Chelsea had gotten here early enough to order an appetizer tray and arrange the newspaper so it was open to the advertisement announcing Bell's grand reopening. It was the first thing Ruby saw when she arrived.

The ad was far more impressive than one would expect from a small-city daily. At first glance, the *Orchard Hill News* offices had looked like something out of an old Clark Gable movie. But Abby, reporter, photographer and miracle worker extraordinaire, had proven that the newspaper was far more than the culmination of steel desks and black phones.

Ruby had designed the ad herself; Abby had suggested a few minor changes. The end result was amazing. Printed on the third page of the local section, the ad was in full color and was undeniably eye-catching, if she did say so herself. There were three water rings on it now and a spot where an appetizer—Chelsea's treat—had dribbled. Ruby had another copy. Okay, three other copies.

The advertisement would run again on Sunday, and then smaller versions would appear each day prior to the Big Night, which was a mere week away. Ruby had butterflies.

She'd been stirring paint for the walls in the ladies' room this morning when Reed had called to ask her if she'd seen the paper yet. He read the ad on his iPad, but she'd put the lid back on the can and walked to the newsstand around the corner while he described it in detail and told her how effective it was. He was right. Nobody could miss it.

She hadn't actually *seen* him since he'd helped her carry the last few boxes of barware into Bell's on Monday, but they'd hit every circuit on the twenty-first century social media network motherboard.

He'd *liked* her online ad. He'd sent her information about a new winemaker in the area on LinkedIn. There had been Tweets and texts. One had read, Anything by Springsteen.

She'd answered, One of my favorites, too, but then so is "Twinkle, Twinkle Little Star," the only song I can still play after three years of piano lessons.

He'd called her to laugh in her ear. That little spot beneath her breastbone had vibrated at the sound of his voice.

A few days later she'd been the one laughing as he'd described the surprise home visit his great-uncle, Judge Ivan-the-Terrible Sullivan, had sprung on Reed and Marsh that day. They'd managed to pass inspection despite the fact that no nanny had been hired as of yet; Joey remained in their care.

"What about Jake Nichols?" Abby cut into Ruby's reverie.

"Who?" Ruby looked at the impossibly forward blonde on the opposite side of the table.

"Jake Nichols is the new veterinarian in town. He's nice-looking and close to six feet tall. He'd probably attend your reunion with you if you asked, as long as you aren't sensitive about the fact that he often smells a little like goats."

Ruby looked to Chelsea for help. "Goats?" Ruby mouthed.

"It's not what it sounds like," Chelsea replied.

Oh. Good? Now where was she? Oh, yes. About the reunion. "I told you," Ruby said to Abby as she speared the last stuffed mushroom on the platter, "I'm attending solo." She was sorry she'd brought up the subject of her class reunion. It was bad enough that Amanda was like a bloodhound on the trail of an escaped convict and wouldn't let the subject rest. Now Abby was on the scent, too.

She tucked a wisp of blond hair behind one ear and said, "Our class reunion was last summer. It was a major hookup fest, let me tell you."

"Oh, great" was all Ruby said. A hookup fest was all she needed.

"Forewarned is forearmed, I always say," Abby insisted.

"I've never heard you say that," Chelsea said.

"That's because no one ever listens to me. Most people don't take petite women seriously. It's true."

"So," Chelsea said, leaning closer to Ruby, pretty

much proving Abby's point. "What does your Peter look like?"

"He's not my Peter."

"He's every girl's *Peter*," Abby countered. "That's the problem."

Ruby dropped her face into her paint-speckled hands.

"You did not just say that," Chelsea reprimanded.

Eye's sparkling with mischief, Abby mouthed, "Sorry."

Chelsea, ladylike no matter the subject matter, turned her violet eyes to Ruby and said, "You don't have to tell us, you know."

With a shrug, Ruby said, "He was covaledictorian, star quarterback, prom king, voted best looking, best dressed, best catch, best you name it."

"How good-looking are we talking?" Abby asked.

Ruby straightened her napkin in her lap and said, "If Jude Law and George Clooney had had a younger brother it would have been Peter Powelson."

"Oh, my," Abby said.

"Oh, dear," Chelsea agreed.

"Tell me about it," Ruby grumbled. "Six-two-and-a-half, thick unruly black hair, cobalt-blue eyes, a washboard stomach, long muscular legs, narrow hips, masculine swagger."

"You thought you'd make beautiful babies together," Abby said on a sigh.

"I was a complete idiot over him. I cried in public over him. And then I practically stalked him. I'm not proud, believe me. It was just— He just…"

"Let me guess," Chelsea said matter-of-factly. "He

told you you changed him in that deep man-place in his soul."

Abby tut-tutted supportively. "And he said it in a midnight-dark whiskey voice and your girl parts did somersaults. Whose wouldn't?"

"That's what I'm afraid of," Ruby said, mashing the innocent stuffed mushroom to smithereens on her own plate. "He wants me back. He's sorry. He insists he's changed. And he's told everyone I know back home that he's going to make his move at the reunion. What if my girl parts, er, you know? I may need a chastity belt."

"You need a date," Abby insisted.

"Yes, well," Ruby said, her gaze straying to the fabulous ad once again. "The reunion's tomorrow night. I'm not seeing anybody, so—"

"Oh," Abby said. "Hi, Marsh, Reed. So this is Joey, isn't it?"

Ruby's gaze swung to the two men who suddenly appeared at the end of her booth. Marsh wore a T-shirt. Reed's button-down was tucked neatly into black slacks. It occurred to her that she'd never seen him in faded jeans and a grimy T-shirt. She wondered what he wore when he relaxed. Did he ever relax?

Marsh held the baby carrier today. Perhaps because the little tyke was at her level, she found herself looking at Joey.

He was dressed in red and white and didn't seem to mind the din of voices and clatter of dishes and silverware. He had a dimple in his chin and an adorable cowlick he was probably going to hate someday. His eyelashes were long and dark—boys always got lashes to die for. He looked everywhere, focusing on nothing, as if in his own little world.

All at once, his gaze landed on Ruby. What followed was a three-and-a-half-month-old's equivalent of a double take. And then it happened. A moment's wonder lit his gray-blue eyes—eyes so like Reed's—his lips twitched and he smiled.

"Hello to you, too," she said.

As if he had a radar lock on her, his grin widened, all gums and round cheeks and sparkling innocence. No wonder Reed was hoping this baby was his. A nagging worry swirled inside Ruby, the tip touching down like the tail of a tornado deep in her chest.

"What are you two doing Saturday night?" Abby was still talking. And Marsh said something Ruby didn't catch.

"What about you, Reed? Are you up to making a former quarterback prom king sorry he ever cheated?"

Ruby did a double take of her own. With a dawning understanding, she said, "Abby." But her voice was still soft from Joey's smile.

She glanced up at the brothers. Marsh looked perplexed, but Reed waited patiently for Abby to continue.

"I'm asking because Ruby's attending her high school class reunion on Saturday, and her ex-boyfriend thinks she's going to let him waltz back into her life, as if he deserves her forgiveness, and, well, she needs a date."

"I do not need—" *Please,* she silently implored Abby. *Do not mention a chastity belt.*

"I might be available," Reed said. And Ruby swore there was a challenge in his voice.

"Great," Abby said. "That's great. Isn't it great, Ruby?"

Since the maiming look Ruby shot Abby had no

noticeable effects, Ruby turned her attention to Reed. "You really don't have to do this."

"That's true, I don't have to."

She tried to look away. Couldn't.

"Will you, though?" Abby asked.

"That depends." A stare-down ensued, and Reed was winning.

Marsh spoke to his brother and then to the three women before he and Joey followed the hostess to a vacant table. Reed stayed behind, holding his ground and Ruby's gaze.

"Well?" he said.

"Do you want me to invite you along, is that it?" she asked.

"*Are* you asking?" he asked.

Her breath caught at his serious expression. Was she? Should she? Did she dare? "I guess I am."

"All right, then," he said.

She thought he might voice some old platitude such as that's what friends are for, or say, "That wasn't so difficult, was it?" Instead, he cast another pointed look directly at her then followed the course Marsh had taken.

There was a noticeable hush at Ruby's table, a pregnant pause straight from an old-fashioned novel, a series of awkward silences that stacked one on top of the other until they teetered precariously, about to topple. Ruby found herself staring at Abby and Chelsea, who were staring back at her in waiting silence.

Finally, Abby whispered, "What was that?"

That, Ruby thought, glancing toward the table near the back of the room where Reed was pulling out a chair, was a polished modern man with a vein of the uncivilized coursing through him. That was the definition of dangerous.

"Apparently," she finally said, "that was my date for tomorrow night."

Ruby jumped out of bed and stubbed her toe. Hobbling now, she supposed that was one way to cure it of any future relentless buzzing. Although, it wasn't her toe that needed curing.

She groped for the bedside table and turned on the lamp. Now that she could see where she was going, she limped to her closet and began to flip through the clothes at the back. If she couldn't sleep, she reasoned, she might as well *do* something.

She already knew exactly what she was going to wear tomorrow night. She'd bought the dress before moving to Orchard Hill, so there would be no surprises, no guesswork. She'd unzipped the garment bag half an hour ago and taken a look. Hanging it on the hook on the back of the closet door, she lowered the zipper again.

The dress was perfect, that was all there was to it—flirty but not too flirty, feminine but not fussy, short but not too short. Perfect. The neckline dipped low in the front but not too low, and a little lower in the back, where she could get away with it. If she were wearing heels and fine jewelry, it might have been too dressy. But she'd found a shabby-chic necklace, a sash belt and the cutest sandals she'd ever seen. The end result was Caribbean casual, like water and air and the sea.

It wasn't over the top. It wasn't too much for a date to her class reunion. Not that it was a real date.

It wasn't.

There was no need to give the dress, the shoes or the jewelry another thought. There was no reason to give her escort for the evening another thought, either.

She crawled back into bed, the fan whirring, night sounds drifting through her screen. She and Reed had touched base earlier via a few strategic texts. She'd given him the banquet center's address and a wide window of time in which to arrive. Since she was part of the welcoming committee and planned to go early to help with last-minute details and he had a very tight schedule, she saw no reason to ask him to arrive when she did. Besides, she was spending the night with her parents, and he would return to Orchard Hill immediately after the reunion was over. Consequently, they were driving separately.

She could hardly believe she was doing this. Amanda was thrilled. Ruby felt…a little breathless. And there, just out of reach again, was that nagging doubt in the back of her mind.

It wasn't as though she was resisting and therefore the zing was persisting. It was— For heaven's sake, she didn't know what it was. She only knew it was midnight and she couldn't sleep for thinking about tomorrow night.

Just then, her phone alerted her to a new text coming in. It was probably Amanda, she thought. Rolling onto her side, she read the new message. Horror flicks or comedies?

She lay on her back again, and smiled. Reed was awake, too.

I live alone, she typed. What do you think?

I would have guessed old classics, he wrote back.

See you in the lobby at the bottom of the stairs at eight.

Smiling again, she turned out the light and settled into her pillows. Maybe she should rethink her shoes. She could always run out tomorrow and buy a pair of decadent heels. Even if Reed hadn't been several inches taller than her, it wouldn't have mattered. Movie stars towered over their escorts all the time. Ruby had never enjoyed leaning down for a good-night kiss. Not that she would kiss Reed. After all, this wasn't a real date. They were just two friends taking turns helping each other.

Liar.

There it was. What was bothering her. A little wish, a fleeting what-if.

What if Joey was Marsh's?

Marsh's, not Reed's.

Then Reed would be free. And there would be no need to resist, no need to pretend that her heart didn't stammer every time she saw him, no need to prepare herself for the possibility that some little blonde bombshell from his past could very well breeze back into his life any day.

She was horrible. No, she wasn't. Okay, maybe she was a little horrible, but in her own defense, it wasn't as if she had the power to change the ultimate outcome of that paternity test. The problem was, for all her good intentions, for all her lack of resisting, her feelings for Reed were deepening.

Whoever turned out to be Joey's father, it would be for the best. She believed that with her whole heart, even though that belief brought a little pang.

She pictured Joey's smile and the way his eyes had

crinkled at the corners. They were like Reed's that way. There it was, that nagging worry again.

Joey had Reed's eyes. Reed's, not Marsh's.

What if Reed really was his father?

Reed Sullivan may have had a vein of the uncivilized coursing through him, but ultimately he was one of those rare individuals who did the right thing no matter what. He would be a wonderful father. Should Cookie return, the fireworks that might have produced Joey could very well be rekindled. Families had been founded on less.

And she, Ruby, would always be a friend, a good friend, but a mere friend, nonetheless.

It would have to be enough. If only it felt like enough.

Ruby had come to Orchard Hill to start over. She was an independent woman and independent women did not need a man.

She was starting to care about Reed, though. Talk about classic.

He'd somehow known her favorite movies were the classics. Lying there listening to the sounds of Division Street in the wee hours of a Saturday morning, she wondered what movie they were most like, her and Reed.

There wasn't any her and Reed. There wasn't, but if there were, which one would it be?

Pride and Prejudice?

That was one of her all-time favorites, but no, she thought, staring at the crack of light shining around the shade at her window. Elizabeth and Mr. Darcy were too proper.

Titanic?

She drew the sheet up to her shoulders. Gosh, no. Too tragic.

Gone With the Wind?

Too epic. She would never be able to pull off a convincing faint. And what about those corsets? Oh, no, Ruby liked to breathe when at all possible.

Casablanca?

She felt dreamy just thinking about that one. She couldn't watch it without putting her hands over her heart. She hoped her life never mirrored it, though. If she ever had another love affair, it would have a happy ending.

She fell asleep thinking Happy Endings would be a good one-of-a-kind-drink title. And she dreamed of a long goodbye.

Chapter Nine

Long goodbyes were not the theme of the evening for the former classmates gathered in the banquet room of Gale, Michigan's, only country club. Boisterous hellos, slaps on the back, squeals of laughter and time-enhanced stories of famed stunts, pranks and adventures abounded.

Ninety-nine young adults had walked across the stage on graduation day ten years ago. There would have been an even one hundred if Cody Holbrook hadn't dropped out two weeks before commencement. Of those ninety-nine, an astounding seventy-one had RSVP'd that they were coming tonight.

By ten minutes before nine, thirty-six of them had asked Ruby, "Is he here yet?"

The he in question was Peter. Not Reed. *He* was stuck in traffic at the Pearl River Bridge, where a semi had reportedly rolled over, and besides, only Amanda, Ruby's absolute BFF, knew about him. Maybe she should have asked him to come earlier, or with her, but it was too late for that. He was driving separately, and he would be here. If not for the traffic jam, he would have been here on time. She was just going to have to be patient a little longer. Unfortunately, patience wasn't her strong suit.

Despite that and the fact that nearly everyone was waiting on pins and needles with bated breath for the highly anticipated promised *scene,* Ruby wasn't having a horrible time. Since she and Amanda were on the planning committee and the welcoming committee, they'd arrived early with name tags for husbands, wives and/or special guests and a Welcome Back Class of 2004 banner.

Most of the football team was in attendance, which explained the state of the hors d'oeuvres table. The once-beautiful arrangement looked as if it had been attacked by pirates or piranhas or both.

Dinner had been served at eight, and now the caterers were clearing the tables and a crowd was forming around the portable bar. Sean Halstead, who'd always been a gifted music fanatic, was supplying the sound track for the evening, and Ruby's brother, Rusty, was keeping an eye out should she decide to take him up on his offer to beat Peter up if he dared show his rakishly handsome face here tonight. Rusty had already blackened Peter's eye after Ruby caught him in bed with someone else, but Ruby forbade a repeat performance.

Secretly, she appreciated his loyalty. Rusty's. Not Peter's. *He* didn't have a loyal bone in his body. Obviously.

Everyone else she'd told, which was practically everybody she knew in Gale, L.A. and Chicago, agreed. It was bad enough that the other woman, a pretty sales rep from Chicago, had been married, but she'd been a *redhead,* too, although not a natural one. Unfortunately, the evidence of that was permanently burned into Ruby's memory.

"Ruby!"

She recognized the stereo of voices calling her name, and was smiling when she turned around. Identical twins Lisa and Livia Holden still dressed alike. Not even Ruby, who'd been on the cheerleading squad with them freshman year, could tell them apart. And she never forgot a face.

Hands up, hair down, smiles gleaming and identical, they yelled, "Give me a *V.* Give me an *I.* Give me a *C.*" And so on until the victory cheer was done.

"Is he here yet?" Lisa, or maybe it was Livia, asked in a normal tone of voice when they were done.

"I wouldn't know." It was Ruby's stock blasé reply. She would have used a similar bland tone if someone had asked if she happened to know who Tom Cruise was dating these days or if she believed aliens had anything to do with building the ancient pyramids. It wasn't that she didn't care at all. She just didn't care very much. Luckily Father Marty was in Rome or she might have had to confess that.

Catherine Ericson, the shyest girl in the class, joined her and Amanda after the twins wandered off to cheer for someone else. "Hey, Ruby," she said.

Ruby and Catherine had been in the drama club together junior year. Catherine's acne had cleared up since then and she'd taken off some weight. She looked quite pretty, but then, she'd always been pretty underneath. Evidently her painful shyness hadn't improved, and she still blushed scarlet. Despite that, she still managed to squeak out *the* question on everyone's mind.

"Is he here yet?"

Bother.

Just then, a hush fell from one end of the room to the other. It didn't require great insight to know what it meant.

He was about to arrive. Peter. Not Reed. She hadn't heard from *him* since a little after nine.

While all eyes were turned toward the door where everyone's favorite tall, dark, handsome and so misunderstood former football star was making his grand entrance, Ruby slipped onto the patio to watch the sun set over the ninth green. Amanda, Evie Carlyle and Violet VanWagner, her closest high school friends and the best posse a girl could ask for, came, too.

It was a warm summer evening. Most of the golfers had headed to the clubhouse, but two remained on the ninth green. One of them missed an easy putt. The cumulus clouds on the horizon concealed all but the faintest shades of coral and lavender tingeing the western sky. Even with the wind whipping Ruby's hair into her eyes, it was still better than witnessing the entire parting of the Red Sea taking place inside.

Ruby, Amanda, Evie and Violet weren't the only ones out here. That was something at least. A small group huddled at the far end, smoking.

Two doors opened onto the broad patio overlooking the green and the Pearl River. Evie was guarding one and Violet the other. Safe for now, Ruby took a fortifying breath.

Beside her, Amanda said, "I'm proud of you for coming tonight. Peter has some nerve. Ninety percent of the people here are hoping you'll forgive him. As *if*."

"You gotta admit," Freddie Benjamin called after passing what was surely a joint to a girl Ruby didn't recognize. "Sending everybody that text. I still love her, man. It was borderline brilliant."

Jason Harding, who'd had a crush on Ruby most of his life, mumbled something, and then said, "You're lookin' good as always, Ruby. You, too, Amanda."

"Thanks, Jason."

"Backatcha, Jase." Wearing four-inch heels and a yellow sundress, Amanda rolled her eyes. In a quieter voice, she said to Ruby, "Missing Peter's grand entrance? Stellar. But you probably aren't going to be able to elude him all night."

It was well after nine by now. Only Ruby knew that the members of Gale High's graduating class of 2004 weren't the only ones who'd received a text from Peter. Ruby's had varied slightly from the others'. I still love you, baby. Give me a chance to prove it. Please.

She was almost afraid to check her phone again.

"He's coming this way," Violet called from her post at the nearest patio door.

"Come on, Ruby! The coast is clear over here," Evie exclaimed.

Ruby's phone vibrated in her hand. Her breath caught as she read the message. Instantly, she started for the door.

"Not this one," Violet called as she neared. "Go through the other door. The one by Evie."

"He's here," Ruby said.

"We know," Violet, who was seven months pregnant, replied. "Peter's heading this way. Half our class is right behind him."

"Not Peter," Ruby said, laying a gentle hand on Violet's baby bump. "Reed."

"Who?"

Leaving Amanda to explain if she so chose, Ruby darted inside on the onrushing breeze, her step light, her dress swirling around her thighs. Her hair, which she'd tamed with large hot rollers hours ago, fell in soft waves down her back.

The serene smile that tipped the corners of her mouth didn't falter as she passed the sea of faces she'd known all her life. Peter, tall and dark and smolderingly confident, was directly ahead of her now.

She blew past him so quickly he probably felt the current of air she left in her wake. A second collective gasp spread through the room just as a Bob Marley song began to play. Once upon a time "Satisfy My Soul" had been their song. Hers and Peter's, back when they had been a "couple." He'd thought of everything.

Darting around the last group of spectators in her way, she burst through the door, the hardwood floor of the banquet room giving way to the soundproof carpet in the hallway. Windows lined one entire wall, flooding the area with fading natural light. The stairs were directly ahead some thirty feet away.

And there, standing at the bottom, was Reed.

Her steps slowed as she neared, stopping altogether when she was six feet away. Behind her, the doors were opening and music and people poured into the hall.

Reed smiled at her. His blond hair was neatly trimmed yet slightly disheveled, his tie in one hand, his collar open at his throat, his pale green shirt a little wrinkled as if he'd been sitting in traffic for a long while.

Ruby didn't know how to proceed. Their "date" had come about only yesterday, and she hadn't talked to him about this. They hadn't rehearsed what they would say or how they would act or what they would do. They were going to have to ad-lib.

He started toward her, his stride long and effortless, and came to a stop less than an arm's length away, close enough to touch her, which he did, his fingers brushing her long hair off her right shoulder. "Maybe later you could tell me what I just missed," he said. "We have an audience, led by some dark-haired guy whose knuckles are dragging on the floor. So if it's all right with you, I think I'll kiss you."

She imagined she must have answered, imagined she knew, somehow, that his kiss would be part of the pseudo-date performance. She imagined that the way she raised her face and the way he lowered his appeared perfectly, exquisitely natural. But the moment his lips touched hers, her mind pulled the curtain on her imagination. Now there was only touch and taste and sound.

She took a small breath and inhaled the scent of warm leather and hot breezes and soap and apples, of all things. Heat shimmered off him, his lips firm and warm on hers, his jaw smooth beneath her fingertips, which meant she must have been touching him. Oh, yes, she was touching him. His skin was taut and slightly rough despite his recent shave, the bones underneath prominent and angular and solid. This wasn't sculpted bronze. This was living, breathing man.

He tilted his head a little, and she opened her lips slightly beneath his. Soft, muted sunset colors floated across her closed eyelids, pale yellow and sky-blue and lavender and coral, which was strange because the windows here faced east not west.

He made a sound deep in his throat. Barely audible, it was deep and dusky and sensual and furthered the sensation of floating.

She'd kissed other men. Some of them were very good at it. In a sense, she and Reed had *resisted* this very activity from the beginning. And yet the pressure of his lips, the way he moved his mouth against hers, his moist breath becoming hers, the taste of him, the feel of him, the fit, all of it felt as if they'd been born to experience this moment.

Her heart pounded, and the kiss changed subtly, like summer sprinkles that gradually gave way to summer rain. It was exploratory, mysterious yet achingly familiar somehow. She'd dreamed last night of a long goodbye. She'd never imagined such a perfectly beautiful long hello.

The kiss ended, stilling like a petal waiting to uncurl until the earth's atmosphere created a drop of dew. They drew slightly apart, their eyes opened, her hand fell away from his face and his fingers uncurled from her hair.

"Wow," she said quietly. "I wasn't expecting that. But wow."

He didn't quite smile.

And a little thrill ran through her, as if she'd done something slightly illicit, or at the very least naughty, and hadn't gotten caught. Actually, she *had* gotten caught, caught by half the graduating class of 2004, caught on at least nine camera phones. More than anything, though, she'd gotten caught up in Reed's kiss.

He took her hand with the first step, and it felt almost as intimate as that kiss. They started across the lobby, fingers twined, their strides smooth and matched. The crowd filtered back inside ahead of them, whispering, wondering what would happen next.

Peter held the door. Ruby wasn't expecting that.

"Who do we have here?" he asked.

She made the introductions and noticed that Reed was taller. Not by much, but a little. She realized it didn't matter. Peter was good-looking; she hadn't been kidding about the Jude Law and George Clooney combination. That didn't matter, either. His eyes were a brilliant blue, although, admittedly, they were tinged with green now.

She wasn't surprised he ignored Reed. That didn't really matter, either, because Reed didn't have to say a word. After all, he was the one who rested his hand lightly on her lower back as they walked through the door.

Behind them Peter was seeing red.

Reed dropped his tie into the first wastebasket he passed. As far as making an impression, he didn't believe a silk tie or anything else could top that kiss. He hadn't planned to do that, but now he didn't see how he could have done anything else. The memory of it had lodged in his bloodstream like a pulse. Ruby had tasted like wine, had sighed like a whisper, had felt tall and willowy and so incredibly soft. It wasn't something a man could forget.

Gale's banquet center was what he'd expected. It had high ceilings, fake pillars, round tables and chairs around the outer edges and a small dance floor on one end. It wasn't a large room, but it comfortably held the hundred or so people present tonight.

The lights weren't bright and the music was a little louder than it needed to be, which nobody seemed to mind. Everyone had to talk louder, but had gotten used to it. Most of them couldn't keep their eyes off Ruby. Reed knew the feeling.

She drew her hand out of his and hugged one of her old classmates the way women often did. It afforded him the perfect opportunity to look at her again.

Whoa had been his first thought when he'd seen her practically flying toward him across the lobby a few minutes ago. Leave it to Ruby to wear white. Not black, not red, not silver or gold. White.

Not a chaste white, either. In fact, it was far from that.

He didn't know a lot about fabric other than that he preferred to wear shirts made of fine cotton. Her dress was soft to the touch, whisper-thin and only slightly heavier than air. The neckline was a gentle sweep from shoulder to shoulder, collarbone to collarbone. It was low enough in the front to show off that delicate hollow at the base of her throat and a few inches of smooth, slightly freckled golden skin below it.

In the back it dipped lower. He didn't see a zipper; he didn't see how she could have gotten into the dress without one. At her waist was a sash in every muted shade of blue and green imaginable. The skirt skimmed her hips, the fabric gathered so softly it flowed like water when she moved. The hem stopped above her knees, quite a few inches above her knees, actually, and on her feet she wore sandals the same color as the beads and shells and pearls stacked one on top of the other around her neck.

Her hair waved loosely down her back. Way down her back. Without the tight curls it was longer than he'd realized. There were other attractive women here tonight. Ruby stole the show. And it wasn't because the most popular guy in the class who'd done her wrong wanted her back, although that appeared to be on everybody's mind. More than that, it was because she knew each and every one of these people. It seemed she'd tried and quit nearly every sport and club she'd joined. She hadn't been kidding when she'd told him she had trouble making up her mind. She'd moved away and come back, fallen for the same guy two or three times and evidently had humiliated herself endearingly. She thought they were all rooting for Peter.

Reed highly doubted that.

She introduced him to her friends, which was practically everyone. Reed knew how to hold his own in any social setting. He smiled and agreed and disagreed when he could do so amicably, but for the most part, he remained at her side, a quiet presence, slightly in the background. This was her party, after all.

There were the usual questions—*How have you been?* and *Where are you living?* and *What do you do?*—a lot of stories and much reminiscing about the good old days. He met her brother, Rusty; her BFF, Amanda; a heavyset friend named Evie and a very pregnant one called Violet.

There was a doctor and a lawyer, a musician and a guy named Freddie who spoke slowly and smelled like weed. And always, Peter laughed a little too loudly and managed to stay a little closer to Ruby than Reed would have liked.

Peter was waiting to make his move. Whether it was retaliation against Reed or an attempted reconciliation with Ruby was anybody's guess.

Leaving Ruby with a group of her friends, Reed waited his turn at the bar. Some guy named Todd talked tax laws with him and another one named Jason Harding looked especially crestfallen. Soon, Reed ordered a Sam Adams for himself and a margarita over crushed ice for Ruby.

Someone to his right nudged him, hard. "You're in my way."

Obviously Ruby's old flame was proud of his shoulders. Taking his half out of the middle, he ordered a Jack Daniel's on the rocks. Something told Reed that Peter worked hard for muscles like his and liked to show them off—arms, shoulders, chest, too, if the way he puffed it out was an accurate indication.

Reed didn't know if Ruby was watching from the other side of the room where he'd left her. He only knew he would have been hard-pressed to mimic Peter's sneer. One thing was certain. The jerk meant to intimidate.

Reed didn't intimidate easily.

"I don't know who you think you are or what you're doing here," Peter began. "Rocky, is it?" As if he didn't know Reed's full name, where he lived, what he drove and how much he earned by now.

Reed shrugged, as if bored. He may not have looked directly at him, but he knew enough from the bar fights he'd gotten caught up in with Noah that it was wise to keep one's potential opponent in his peripheral vision at all times.

"I'm sure you've heard I hurt her," he said bitterly, swirling his whiskey in his glass.

"Actually," Reed finally said, "Ruby has told me very little about you."

The bartender smirked. And so did the CPA and the shorter guy with the spaniel eyes. Score one for Reed.

"Yes, well," Peter the Great said with his customary sneer. "It's not surprising, given the fact that she only moved away two weeks ago. How well could you possibly know her?"

It looked to everyone within hearing range that this point would go to Peter. Reed took a drink from his longneck bottle. "And yet I'm the one she's with tonight."

Ha.

Score another point for Reed.

"You do not want to get in a pissing match with me, pal."

The pal rankled. Ruby had called him that more than once.

"You're right about that," Reed said, his Sam Adams in one hand and Ruby's margarita now in the other. "As far as I can see, there is no match. Skeeter, is it?"

The unofficial score was three to zip by the time Reed returned to the spot where he'd left Ruby five minutes ago. She wasn't there, though. In fact, he didn't see her anywhere in the room, and Ruby O'Toole stood out in a crowd.

A patient man, he stayed at the edge of the dance floor. Quietly nursing his beer, he waited for the belle of the ball to return.

Chapter Ten

The door swished shut quietly behind Ruby as she left the lounge. Someone had dimmed the lights in the hallway and in the adjoining banquet hall. Letting her eyes adjust, she paused for a moment and looked around. She didn't see Reed anywhere.

She'd planned only a quick visit to the ladies' room to run a comb through her hair and reapply her lip gloss. She should have known better than to underestimate what hubs of social activity women's restrooms could be, especially when there was an adjoining lounge with velvet settees and slipper chairs.

Since almost no one was dancing, the only location boasting more activity right now was the bar. She didn't see Reed there, either, though. Actually, she didn't see him by the punch table or the hors d'oeuvres table or with the small group made up of guests who didn't know anybody else. Maybe he was visiting the men's room. For guys, those were always quick trips, just one of the many differences in the sexes.

Wherever he was, she wondered if his ears had been ringing while she'd been gone. Funny, she'd expected everyone to ask about Peter. Instead, they were more curious about Reed.

Many of their questions had easy answers, which she'd readily given. She'd met him her second day in Orchard Hill. Yes, he was tall. No, not six-five, more like six-three. Yes, he was good-looking, too.

And okay, while they were on the subject, no, she hadn't shrunk, she was still five-ten and three-quarters, and she hadn't lost weight, either. No, she didn't know where he bought his clothes. Yes, yes, yes, he wore them well.

His shoes did look expensive, and no, she didn't know his shoe size. He'd gone to Purdue, and she didn't think he'd ever been married, and his eyes were dreamy, weren't they?

She'd hedged the more intimate queries, and at times she simply smiled. She couldn't help it if there was a dreamy depth in her eyes and a secret knowledge in what she didn't say. She was having a wonderful time, after all; she felt a glow deep inside, and it seemed to have started with that kiss.

Here in the banquet hall, Peter was talking to two friends from the old football team, Chad Wilson and Tripp Donahue. Although she pretended she hadn't noticed, she'd felt Peter looking at her much of the evening. His impressive biceps and trim waist, all that dark whisker stubble and those smoldering cobalt eyes were impossible to miss. He'd been part of the raucous group who'd drunk to the winning touchdown, his, that had earned the team a trophy and a permanent place behind glass in the display case outside the cafeteria at school. Once or twice she'd returned his smile. She wondered if he realized yet that it didn't mean anything.

It was getting late; everyone had to vacate the premises by midnight, which wasn't bad for a town that normally rolled up its sidewalks by nine. More guests were leaving all the time. Amanda was dancing with her fiancé, Todd; Violet and her husband had gone home a while ago. Evie, that little seductress, had ducked out with Max Hamilton, and Livia Holden was leaving this very minute with Jack Simon—or was that Lisa? Ruby never could tell those two apart. Rumor had it that Eric Gordon had sneaked out with someone else's date.

Abby and Chelsea had been right. Class reunions were major hookup fests.

Ruby hadn't given Peter his moment in the spotlight yet. She knew him, though, and any minute now he was going to take matters into his own hands.

She saw a movement across the room. Brock Avery, Gale High's former basketball center, and his girlfriend, a model named Fowler, just Fowler—that Brock always had been able to pick them—took a seat opposite the most-talked-about outsider here tonight.

There sat Reed, looking interested in whatever Brock and Fowler were saying. His pale green shirt was still tucked in, the sleeves now rolled up a few times at his forearms, elbows on the table, feet apart, one leg stretched out comfortably, basically a naturally delicious slice of man.

He laughed at something Fowler said, listened, said something in return. And so the exchange went.

It looked as if he was drinking a Sam Adams, but it could have been a Bud Light for all she cared. It wasn't his choice of beer that sent that interesting little flutter through her chest.

The bottle was halfway to his mouth when he turned his head and saw her. She started toward him, and even though his table wasn't far away, he was on his feet before she reached it. She wondered who'd instilled those incredible manners. Or were all Sullivans predisposed to fine conduct?

The O'Tooles, not so much, which Ruby demonstrated upon reaching Reed's side. Having already spoken to Brock and his gorgeous girlfriend, Ruby smiled in their general direction and looked up at Reed. "Is that margarita for me per chance?"

His chin came down just a little, and so did his eyelids. It was a dreamy expression, one that made her think about dreamy activities, bedroom activities.

"It's yours," he said, his voice low. "The ice melted. I can get you a fresh one if you'd like."

She shook her head and took a sip of the cool watery drink. "The place is clearing out. I didn't mean to be gone so long."

"Did you solve the nuclear crisis and discover a cure for the common cold?"

She took another sip, and another. "We're close, very close. Did you really call Peter Skeeter?"

Taking the drink from her hand, he placed it on the table next to his and said, "That's for me to know and you to find out. Do you hear that?"

Nodding, she remembered when he'd told her his favorite music was anything by Springsteen. "Was this song a personal request?"

"No, but I believe my patience is finally being rewarded." He took her hand and drew her with him onto the dance floor.

Stopping in a roomy spot, he faced her. They each took a step, meeting in the middle, her hand curling against his, his warm fingers lacing with her cool ones.

She'd taken dance in college. She could waltz, rumba, tango, jitterbug, and yes, she could even do the Macarena. Reed may not have known all those dances, but he knew enough to move his feet. And he knew where to put his other hand.

"You do realize," she said, close to his ear, "your touch is below proprietary and only slightly above Neanderthal."

He tightened his hold at the small of her back and drew her slightly closer. "Exactly where every guy in this room would like to be."

His voice was a low rumble, a quiet vibration that found its way into her ear, spreading in every direction, rippling outward and inward, pausing in unconnected places beneath her collarbone and breastbone, below her navel, bubbling like a science experiment along the insides of her hip bones before finally reaching her very center. She was still relishing the possibilities when someone tapped Reed on the shoulder.

Peter was cutting in.

Reed stiffened. Ruby did, too, and glanced from one man to the other. One was dark, the other fair, one determined, the other reluctant.

"It's all right, Reed," she said, and released her held breath. "Hello, Peter."

There was another moment's awkwardness, and then, his mouth set in a firm line, Reed nodded at Ruby, stepped back and let her go. With an indecipherable smile, she went from Reed's arms to Skeeter's—er, Peter's.

It was going to rain.

Reed knew the weather. He recognized the different cloud patterns, felt the shifting air currents and understood atmospheric pressure. The wind was changing.

Prophetic, perhaps.

It was going to rain. He could smell it, feel it, taste it. He tasted blood, too, but that was from nearly biting through his cheek.

He put a hand to the back of his neck. And forced himself to breathe.

From the dance floor he'd come directly to the patio. He couldn't claim to have refrained from looking back; but he'd looked back only once. Of the few dozen people still here, half had been watching him and all were probably wondering if they were going to get their promised scene, after all.

Lover Boy had had all night to make his move. Yet he'd waited until the deejay with the impressive sound system finally, *finally* put on a song by Springsteen. That rankled to beat hell.

Reed didn't relish the picture in his mind of Ruby deep in conversation with Tall, Dark and Handsome, *his* hand on her lower back now. They looked a little too cozy. Intimate.

Hell.

She didn't need Reed's protection. It was the honest-to-God truth. She was independent, self-reliant and would know where to slam her knee should the need arise. Besides, every guy here would come to her aid,

and half the women, too. Peter Powelson may have
been their former football star, but Ruby was everyone's friend.

The party was almost over. Reed didn't know how
he felt about that.

He hadn't attended his ten-year class reunion five
years ago. He didn't remember what excuse he'd given.
He hadn't kept in close contact with most of the members of his graduating class. At the time, he'd been deep
in negotiations to supply four varieties of fresh apples
from Sullivans Orchard to the second-largest grocery
chain in Michigan. Also there had been talk of an apple
pickers' strike, the cider house had been getting a new
roof and, as always, there had been hiring and firing
and renovations and expansion and upkeep on buildings and equipment. And, of course, Noah and Marsh
and Madeline had needed tending to. The truth went a
little deeper than work or family obligations. He hadn't
kept in close contact with members of his graduating
class because he hadn't wanted to have to try to explain why he wasn't living in Miami or Seattle or, hell,
Timbuktu. He hadn't wanted their pity. So he'd never
given them a chance to understand.

Somehow, Ruby had figured it out. She'd put two
and two together, and simply accepted that sometimes
people's lives changed, and sometimes their lives
changed them. She didn't pity him. She respected his
choice, as he did, and that made him feel ten feet tall.
Respect fed a man's soul. Perhaps even more dangerous, it made him feel understood.

He wondered what was happening on that dance
floor. But she didn't need any more of an audience, and

he didn't care to witness Peter's heartfelt, heartrending, soul-baring, deeply moving final play.

So as "Born to Run" wound down—why the hell it had to be Springsteen, he didn't know—as the last notes played, Reed stood on the patio overlooking an empty green and a meandering river, both lit by modernized antique gas lanterns on iron posts. He didn't put on a superhero cape or pound his chest with his fists. Instead, he let the most beautiful woman he'd ever known, the kindest and funniest and most capable, too, decide if she wanted to give a man she'd once loved another chance.

Reed fervently hoped she didn't. He fervently hoped Lover Boy didn't kiss her.

He wanted to be the one doing that.

"Mmm. Smell that?" Ruby asked as she and Reed strolled to his Mustang at the far end of the parking lot.

Finally, the reunion was over, and everyone except Sean Halstead, who was loading up his speakers, woofers, tweeters, microphones and the rest of his equipment this very minute, had already left. Not daring to let go of her dress for more than half a second in this wind, Ruby quickly waved to Amanda and Todd as they drove away.

"Reed? I was just wondering if you smelled that," she repeated.

"Asphalt?" he asked.

She nudged him with her elbow. The country club must have resurfaced the parking lot recently. It did smell of asphalt. That wasn't what she meant. Rain was in the air, but that wasn't what she meant, either. She was going to say it was the scent of happiness.

This was the second time she'd walked across this parking lot since the reunion had wound down. The first time she'd agreed to come out here with Peter. By the time Peter had driven away and she'd gone back inside, Reed had been talking to Sean while he packed up his computer and speakers and other music paraphernalia.

Since she'd ridden to the banquet hall with Amanda, Ruby had asked Reed earlier if he'd mind dropping her at her parents'. Although he'd said he'd be happy to, she hadn't actually talked to him since their last dance.

"Are you wondering what I said to Peter?" she asked.

"Who?" he said.

The wind whipped her hair across her face and there wasn't a thing she could do about it because it took both hands to hold her dress down.

"Okay," he finally said. "If you insist upon telling me, fine. Go ahead."

She smiled wryly. "That's for me to know."

His answering smile looked as if it might just crack his face. He'd been an amazing sport tonight. She had no idea how to thank him.

She'd been dreading this reunion. Everyone in that room had heard the entire sordid tale of how she'd let herself into Peter's apartment that day in April. She'd planned to leave him a seductive note, a red rose and— she was loath to admit this—her panties. Not the pair she'd been wearing, but a darling little see-through thong she'd purchased at Victoria's Secret especially for her escapade. She'd tried to wear a similar scrap of elastic and lace once, but such panties were strictly seduction ploys. Of course they came off easily. Who could stand to wear them?

Peter had been wining and dining her ever since they'd both found themselves back in Gale right after Christmas. She'd gone to work for her father and Peter had taken a position in hospital administration in nearby Traverse City. He'd been especially amorous of late, and that day she'd planned to leave the rose, the note and those panties on Peter's pillow.

She heard something upon closing his door, but it was an apartment, and she assumed the muted voices were coming from the neighbors. She'd actually felt a feverish and giddy sense of excitement as she'd tiptoed toward his bedroom. Odd that he kept the door closed when he wasn't home, but she opened it easily with a gentle turn of the handle.

The red rose and the note and—truth be told—the poorest excuse for underwear in the world fell to the floor where she stood just inside his bedroom. Instead of getting to leave her gifts on it, Peter's pillow had been propped under some other woman's hips. Not that that little detail registered at first. At that point all she could focus on was the woman's ankles crossed at the back of Peter's neck.

Ruby must have gasped.

And Peter had looked over his shoulder, giving her access to certain things she didn't want to see. Ruby remembered someone swearing—her—and someone calling her name—Peter. That was all she remembered, because that was when she spun around and let herself out. Of his bedroom, of his apartment, and eventually, out of his life.

Walking next to Reed tonight, she realized that Peter

hadn't been the right guy for her. Oh, he was tall and had beautiful eyes and wonderful pecs and washboard abs. Sure, he liked to show his muscles off in tight shirts, or better yet, no shirt.

He'd cheated.

Cheated.

And she'd become one of *those* women. Those wronged souls who blamed themselves for their partners' infidelity. For surely there must have been something wrong with Ruby, with her kisses or her lovemaking. Why else would Peter have strayed? For weeks afterward, she'd shown up at his favorite haunts, drove past his apartment and the hospital where he worked. She was a pathetic crybaby who hid under the produce stand at Meijer and plotted how she might win him back.

As if he was somehow worthy. As if she needed him in order to ever be happy again.

What happened to the girl who'd tried out for every sports team and joined—okay, and also quit—every club in school? What happened to the fiery young woman who took chances and made mistakes but in the process took a stand?

Tonight, laughing with old friends about old times, she'd looked across the room and found Reed looking back at her. And she'd discovered not the girl she'd been, not the woman she wanted to be, but the woman she already was.

Reed liked her. Simply. Truly. Liked. Her.

She'd seen it in his eyes.

Nothing was unforgivable, she'd told Peter a few minutes ago. Before his smile had gotten too cocky, she'd finished her statement. "But I don't love you enough anymore to find the energy it would take to work this relationship out, to learn to trust you again. That's too great a learning curve. It would take too much of *me* and there just wouldn't be enough of me left."

She was back to her old self. Only better. And now she really needed to let Reed get back to Orchard Hill and his life and reality. She wished there was some way to let him know how much she appreciated his show of confidence tonight, his quiet presence. He'd called Peter Skeeter. She would have loved to have been a fly on that wall. Just because she liked herself again didn't mean she was perfect.

"What's so funny?" The consummate gentleman, Reed opened the passenger door for her.

"Oh, nothing," she said. "Everything."

"It's good that you've narrowed it down."

The breeze had turned cool. It was the kind of late-night breeze that smelled of summer and asphalt and hinted of rain, the kind that caused people to stop what they were doing and tip their faces up and hold their arms out simply to feel it more fully. It was the kind of breeze that only occurred after midnight, the kind that made Ruby ask, "Did you just feel a raindrop?"

"For the last ten minutes," he said.

She smiled up at him, her hair swirling. He looked down at her, his shirt collar fluttering. She touched his arm. "I just want you to know," she said, "I'll never forget what you did for me tonight."

"Ruby," he said, his voice whisper-soft.

They would never know for sure who started it or how it began. One moment their gazes were locked. The next moment their lips were.

They met on a surge of heat and unbridled desire. They'd kissed before. Once. This was different. It was wild, unplanned but necessary. It was lips and tongues and breaths and moans and then all of those all over again. Ruby hadn't intended to do this, neither of them had. She hadn't meant to let the wind have its way with her skirt or for Reed to have his way with her mouth.

And yet the wind blew and the kiss swirled and a wild stampeding had started in her chest. His hands were all over her back, up and down and high and low, molding her to him. Hers were in his hair, gliding to his shoulders, pressing his chest, where his heart was stampeding just like hers.

Thunder rumbled in the distance. He groaned in answer deep in his throat, and the kiss became a mating of lips and tongues and the very wind that spun all around them. It went on and on and might have gone on forever.

But it couldn't, and finally, somehow, he dragged his mouth from hers. "Ruby."

"I know," she rasped close to his ear.

"I want to."

"I know," she said again. "So do I."

"But I can't. We can't. Not until I know. Maybe never. I can't ask you to wait. I can't do this."

"I know," she whispered. "I do. It's for the best. It is."

He drew away slightly, just a few inches, and looked at her, his storm-cloud blue-gray eyes meeting her desire-hazed green ones. And then his lips were on hers and hers were on him and his hands were on either side of her face and her palm was pressed against his chest, heat radiating off him in waves, his heart galloping beneath her fingertips.

The next time, *she* broke away. "Reed."

He groaned.

"We have to stop."

He touched his forehead to hers. "Yes, we do. You're beautiful. You're amazing. You're right."

Her hands went to his face, and then she was pulling him back to her, his lips to hers. His arms wrapped around her all over again, and he lifted her off her feet, pressing her backward against the solid car, levering himself against her.

If it were possible to make love through their clothes, they would have. He was hard where she was soft, and they both strained toward more, each in their own way, one seeking, the other wanting with everything she had.

Luckily, it wasn't possible. Although it didn't feel like luck. It felt like frustration and barriers they would have just as soon surmounted.

Still, they couldn't make love. They wouldn't make love. They didn't.

What they did instead was take deep breaths and return to reality. Bit by bit, with a little awkwardness and great reluctance they untangled their hands and arms and she unwound her legs from around his waist and he set her back on her feet.

"I'd better get you home," he said.

She pushed her hair out of her face and slipped into the car. He closed the door and went around to the driver's side, climbed behind the steering wheel and turned the key.

For the first time in her life, she wished Gale were

a little larger. As it was, it took about two minutes to drive to her parents' house on Bridge Street, where she was spending the night.

Cinderella's coach had turned back into a pumpkin at midnight. Ruby's fairy-tale evening was ending in a similar way, but closer to one.

Reed didn't look at Ruby during the drive over streets in need of resurfacing, like so many other streets in towns all across America these days. Other than her giving him brief directions, they didn't speak. He concentrated on his driving, and did what he could to ignore the desire that had settled low and solid at his very core.

He couldn't forget the way she'd felt in his arms, pliant and warm and willing and so incredibly beautiful. He shouldn't have let things get that far out of control. And yet he'd been imagining it ever since he'd finally driven out of that traffic jam on the Pearl River Bridge, ever since he'd arrived at the reunion, ever since he'd seen Ruby rushing toward him in that white dress, her long red hair and blue-and-green sash flying behind her.

As far as he knew, she didn't look at him during the drive, either. Neither of them attempted small talk.

He could see a few sprinkles in the low beams of his headlights. The wind was still strong, but the clouds hadn't given up much rain yet.

She unfastened her seat belt before he'd brought the car to a complete stop in her parents' driveway. He threw the shift lever into Park and undid his. Whatever she'd been going to say went unsaid as she got out, as if she knew it would be a waste of breath to tell a Sullivan she would see herself to her door.

They met at the front of his car, the glow of headlights shining low and the porch light shining bright. "I've got it from here," she said at the bottom of the porch steps.

"What did you say to Lover Boy, anyway?" he asked.

She rolled her eyes, and he knew it would be a cold day in hell before she ever relayed the exchange to anyone word for word. It broke the awkwardness, though, so he wasn't sorry he'd asked.

"You're beautiful, Ruby. Outside and in."

"Good night, pal."

He watched her go up the steps. She was reaching for the screen door when his phone rang.

He grabbed the cell and looked at the screen. It was almost 1:00 a.m. And it was Marsh. Something had to be wrong.

Reed pressed the button and heard his brother say, "There's someone here who wants to talk to you."

"What?" Reed asked a little too loudly.

The next voice he heard was soft and sultry and decidedly Southern. "Reed, honey?"

"Who is this?"

"It's me. Cookie."

"What? Who?" he asked. "Did you say this is Cookie?" He had to listen hard in order to hear her confirm it. "Where are you?" He listened again, and like the parrot he'd obviously become, he repeated, "You're at the orchard? In Orchard Hill?"

"I came back for our baby, sugarplum."

"You came for Joey?" His gaze went unbidden to

the porch, and he saw Ruby's hand fall away from the door. She turned to face him as Cookie rattled off what sounded like some sort of explanation. The connection was terrible and his own heartbeat was so loud in his ears he couldn't hear most of what she said. "Put Marsh back on, would you?" he finally managed to rasp.

His brother's voice vibrated with the same intensity Reed was feeling. "I put her suitcases in the spare room."

In other words, she wasn't leaving with Joey tonight. Thank God for that. "I'm on my way," Reed said.

"We'll be waiting. Hey, Reed. The radar shows rain. Heavy rain. Drive carefully. I've got things covered until you get here."

The connection broke, and Reed's hands fell to his sides, his gaze on Ruby. She stood on her parents' front porch, the soft overhead light washing her in a golden glow. Or maybe that was his imagination.

He wasn't imagining the quaver in her voice, though, as she said, "That was Cookie?"

Nodding, he felt as if he owed Ruby an explanation, and yet he had no idea what protocol to follow. "Marsh said she showed up out of the blue insisting she'd made a terrible mistake."

The wind whipped Ruby's hair off her forehead and pressed her dress to her thighs as she held her skirt with one hand. She doubted Reed would leave until she was safely inside. The entire night felt surreal, somehow, and yet she knew she would never forget the way he was looking at her.

The low beam of his headlights cast his shadow onto the porch steps. She'd seen that stance before, feet apart, back straight, shoulders squared. With the light behind him, she couldn't see the color of his eyes. She felt his gaze, though. It was as if his fingers were actually trailing across her cheek, down her neck, across her shoulder, along her arm, to her waist.

She had no right to respond, and yet she did, warming, wishing, wanting. He'd called it the zing. It was more than that, at least for her.

He stared at her, and she at him, and neither of them knew what to say. She swallowed the lump in her throat as one thought played over and over in her mind. In one night she'd gotten over a man who would always cheat, and fallen in love with one who never would.

Oh, the irony.

Chapter Eleven

The storm raged as Reed left Ruby's hometown.

Even with his windshield wipers on high, he could barely see. Semis were parked along the side of the road and cars waited out the storm beneath overpasses. Slowing to a crawl at times, he kept both hands on the steering wheel, pressing toward home.

Rain came down in sheets, thunder boomed and lightning forked out of the sky. Not even the raging storm could keep him from thinking about what he'd just left behind and what he would soon encounter back home.

He drove out of the storm sometime after two. In the back of his mind he made a list of questions he would ask Cookie. He wasn't sure what to expect, but for the next hundred miles, Reed thought about what he would say, how he would say it and how it would feel if Cookie was indeed the mother of his son. On the one hand, it would mean Joey was his, and Reed deeply wanted that. It had seemed straightforward a few weeks ago. Nothing felt simple tonight.

His clothes were still damp when he pulled into his own driveway just after four o'clock. Steering around the fallen limb lying across his path, he parked where he always parked. His feet splashed through the residual puddles on the sidewalk as he went up the back steps and let himself in.

A television was turned low to an all-night weather station. Joey wasn't crying. So far so good.

There was a quarter pot of coffee left in the coffeemaker, the seldom-used sugar bowl was out and two mugs and an empty baby bottle sat by the sink.

The night-light was on in the nursery where Joey slept during the day. The crib was empty.

Feeling the effects of the long day and an even longer night that had no end in sight, Reed ran a hand through his hair and continued toward the soft murmur of voices in the living room. One belonged to his brother. The other one was vaguely familiar, as well.

Marsh was sitting in his favorite chair, his feet bare, his jeans ripped across one knee, his fingers strumming the cracked leather on the armrest, looking for all the world like something the cat dragged in. He jumped up the instant he saw Reed.

But Reed wasn't looking at Marsh anymore. His eyes were trained on a woman he hadn't seen in more than a year.

She wore pink jeans and a formfitting shirt. Her shoes, the right one tipped onto its side, sat on the floor next to the sofa. Her hair was a little longer than he remembered and perhaps lighter, too, but her eyes and smile were the same.

It was her, all right.

"Hello, Reedykins." With a bat of her eyelashes, she rose sinuously to her feet. "If you aren't a sight for sore eyes. It's been a while, hasn't it?"

His first coherent thought was that she could stand, and walk, and talk. She wasn't paralyzed or otherwise incapacitated, which was just one possible reason that might have forced a woman to leave a baby on a man's doorstep. He also couldn't think of any good reason for her to have kept their child's very existence a secret until two and a half weeks ago.

"Where's Joey?" he asked.

Her eyes widened innocently. "Why, he's in bed, of course. It's after four, you know."

Yes, Reed knew.

"Y'all must have a million questions." She was including Marsh now with her tender, quivering little smile.

Looking pointedly at Reed, Marsh said, "You two have a lot to talk about. I think I'll turn in." He started toward the kitchen and ultimately the back stairs.

There was an open staircase in this very room. With Marsh's selection of the other one, Reed knew his brother wanted him to follow him into the kitchen, where they might have a moment of privacy.

"Would you excuse me for a minute?" Reed said to Cookie.

"Of course, sugar. Take all the time you need." She sank back into the soft leather sofa cushion and curled her feet underneath her.

Marsh was waiting for him in the kitchen. "It is her, then?"

"It's the woman I— Uh, yeah. It's her. Did she tell you anything?"

Marsh put both hands on his head as if to prevent an explosion. "She's talkative, all right."

Reed remembered that about her. In fact, it was one of the reasons he'd kissed her the first time.

Marsh wasn't the type to elaborate. Sometimes getting information out of him was like pulling teeth. "Did she mention why she left Joey or why she came back now?" Reed asked.

Marsh shook his head. "She never got around to that, but Cookie isn't a nickname. And her last name is Nelson."

"How is she with Joey?" Reed asked very, very quietly.

"She hasn't seen him yet."

Reed met his brother's gaze. That didn't make sense. Finally he said, "Has she asked about him at all?"

It was Marsh's turn to sigh. "I offered to show her where he sleeps, but she said she didn't want to disturb him."

"Do you think she's telling the truth?" Reed whispered.

"About not wanting to disturb him? Hell, how should I know?" The refrigerator clanked on and the predawn breeze rattled the blinds at the kitchen window. Marsh scratched his stubbly jaw and yawned. "If you mean is she telling the truth about being Joey's mother, she offered to show me her stretch marks. No, I did not take her up on it. This is your baby."

Reed didn't miss his brother's grimace at the double entendre. He wanted Joey to be his as badly as Reed did, for his own good reasons.

"The truth is," Reed said quietly, "we don't know any more right now than we knew before she arrived. I left a message for Sam, but until we have proof, let's not let Joey out of our sight."

Marsh's relief was palpable.

Feeling an enormous surge of affection and gratitude for his brother, Reed said, "Hopefully we'll be able to fill in the blanks after I've spoken with Cookie. Meanwhile, I'll take this watch. Get some sleep."

"I think I'll do that." Marsh started to go, stopped. "How was the reunion?"

Reed thought about Ruby's friends and her laughter and how she'd contributed to all the newsy, breezy conversations, all the remember-whens, what-are-you-doing-nows. Ruby O'Toole put the joy in enjoyment.

He thought about Springsteen and how it had felt to see her dancing in Skeeter's arms. He thought about walking her to the car and the wind in her hair and his mouth on hers, and how the thrum of her kisses, her touch and her sighs was still in his bloodstream.

"It was fine. I had an okay time."

Marsh looked at him. And Reed very nearly groaned at the understatement.

His brother would never call him on it. That wasn't Marsh's way. He started up the stairs. Reed imagined he would stop at Joey's door, but he didn't have time to think about that right now. Instead, he retraced his footsteps to the living room for a little one-on-one with Cookie.

He noticed she wasn't sitting up anymore. He went as far as the center of the room and called her name. "Cookie?"

Her eyes were shut, her breathing quiet. Curled up on one end of the large sofa, she appeared to be sleeping.

"Cookie?" he said more sternly.

Her eyes remained closed and her chest rose and fell evenly, calling attention to her— Several terms came to mind, but he refused them all and turned his attention back to her face. She had a small round face, a narrow nose, lots of hair and fake eyelashes. She was cute—pretty, actually.

What game was she playing? Or did she have a good reason for her actions?

"Cookie, can you hear me?"

Nothing. Bending over her, he reached for her shoulder, only to pause, his hand suspended several inches above her. "Cookie?" he said louder than ever.

She didn't move a muscle.

"Cookie, wake up." He gave her shoulder a little shake. She was as limp as a rag doll. He tried again. All she did was sigh.

"Cookie, come on. Get up." If there was ever a time when he might take up swearing, it was now. He'd driven for hours through a torrential downpour, past downed trees and power lines, past accidents and flashing lights. The least she could do was sit the hell up and talk to him, dammit.

It was no use. Evidently one of those people who could sleep through a train wreck, she was out cold.

Straightening, he put his hand to his forehead, where tension was trying to expand his skull from the inside. The woman had one hell of a lot of explaining to do. He looked at her again and considered his options. Carrying her upstairs to the spare room did not appeal to him, and he didn't see what good it would do to sit here twiddling his thumbs while she slept. He faced the inevitable. His questions were going to have to wait.

Feeling as though he was suddenly all thumbs, he drew a plaid throw over her and turned out all but one lamp. Casting one last look over his shoulder, he went upstairs to bed.

He stopped in the doorway of Noah's old room. Light from the hallway stretched almost to the crib, where Joey was sound asleep. The floor creaked in the usual places as Reed went in and closed the door. He took off his shoes and peeled out of his damp clothes. After donning one of Noah's T-shirts and an old pair of sweats, he stretched out on Noah's old bed.

Noah's airplane posters were still tacked to the walls, and yet the room smelled of baby, milky and sweet and innocent somehow. Joey made little humming noises in his sleep, his breathing soft and fluttery. Utterly peaceful, this innocent baby had no idea his mother had returned.

If Cookie was his mother, that is.

Odd that she hadn't wanted to hold him after being away from him for nearly a month. Maybe she *was* exhausted from traveling, but even if she were dead on her feet, wouldn't she have wanted—needed—to at least check on him, to see him with her own two eyes, to prove that he was okay? Maybe she wasn't a good mother.

Or maybe he was looking for flaws.

The floors at Bell's looked fabulous. Everything was fabulous. Wonderful.

Peachy.

Ruby propped the tavern's back door open with a

chair to air out the lingering, unpleasant smell of poly-urethane, and caught herself wondering how things were going at Reed's house. Oh no she didn't. She wasn't going to think about Reed and Cookie. Or Reed with Cookie. She closed her eyes because telling her-self she wasn't going to think about it only made her think about it more.

She'd arrived back in Orchard Hill yesterday after-noon. She hadn't heard from Reed since he'd driven away from her parents' house. She hadn't texted him, or vice versa. She had no reason to. And vice versa.

All that kissing had pretty much made the friendship connection null and void. Perhaps some women could just be friends with a man they were in love with, but not Ruby. Unrequited love wasn't her style.

She had no one to blame but herself and even that wasn't doing any good. So. There was no sense wast-ing her time thinking about a few kisses and what had almost been. It was already Monday and she had too much to do to while away her time on what-ifs.

Later today she was interviewing her last candidate for bartender. In a pinch, Ruby could bartend, but she hoped that wouldn't be necessary. She planned to print and laminate the menu next, and then she would apply a coat of beeswax to the bar. And there were about a hundred other tasks to complete in preparation for the grand reopening of Bell's Tavern.

Most everything was on track. The shelves were stocked and her new waitstaff was ready to begin. The cash drawer had a lock, and she'd hired a short-order cook as well as a local band for Friday night. The full-size ad had run again in Sunday's paper and a smaller version had appeared in today's edition. Her online ads had garnered a great deal of excitement, too.

She wished she were more excited.

Hoping to generate a little cross breeze, she propped the front door open, too. She wondered if Joey remembered his mother, wondered if he'd sighed when he was finally in her arms again, home at last. She wondered if there'd been any fireworks yet. Not that she was worried about that. Why would she worry when she wasn't even thinking about Reed? Or Cookie. Or Reed and Cookie. Or Reed with Cookie.

She sighed, for all her determination couldn't seem to keep Reed far from her thoughts.

Methodically attacking the remaining items on her to-do list, she carried the Welcome to Bell's Grand Reopening banner to the front window. The moment she got there, it became clear to her that she had the worst timing in the world.

Reed was walking by.

She hadn't seen him in two days, which, from the looks of him, was how long it had been since he'd shaved. He was carrying Joey. The two of them appeared to be alone. She simply couldn't help wondering what had happened when he'd come face-to-face with Cookie.

Where was she, anyway?

He happened to be walking by, and he happened to look tired and slightly bedraggled. Ruby refused to drink in the sight of him. And she refused to duck and hide. She'd done that during the Cheater Peter debacle and she vowed she would never humiliate herself that way again.

Also, Reed had already seen her.

She definitely had the worst timing in the world. He didn't appear to think so, for his expression changed. He stopped and looked at her, and she swore he was glad to see her. Ruby had trouble drawing a breath. And yet she found herself reacting, her face relaxing, a smile lurking. The courthouse clock chimed on the quarter hour, two minutes late, as usual. They both smiled, and they might as well have been back in that parking lot after midnight, the wind whipping and rain threatening and their bodies warm and growing warmer all the time.

She supposed she shouldn't have been surprised he wandered inside. The front door was wide open, after all. It wasn't as if they were strangers or adversaries. She wasn't sure what they were anymore. Not just friends. Not lovers.

Joey's eyes widened adorably now that he was out of the sun. Reed's adjusted faster, blue-gray pools of appeal beneath sandy-colored brows.

"Hi," he said.

"Hey," she said at the same time.

A moment of awkwardness followed. And then he said, "We're meeting Marsh and Sam for coffee at the Hill in a few minutes."

We? Ruby thought. "Why is Sam still in town?" she asked.

He met her gaze. "There are some unanswered questions."

Which could have meant anything. Since it was followed by another unwieldy pause, she could only assume it meant something important. "Unanswered questions regarding Cookie?"

"Yes." He didn't elaborate, and she didn't feel she

had the right to ask. Odd, since she'd had no qualms about asking him anything. But that was before.

Before they'd kissed. Before she'd fallen in love with him. Before Cookie breezed into town on the tail of a storm.

Was Cookie Joey's mother? she wondered. Or wasn't she? Was she still in town? What reasons did she give for leaving him? For returning for him now? Ruby couldn't ask any of those questions, so she settled for something safe. "Does this banner show up from outside?"

Since he couldn't very well say what he was thinking, either, he said, "It does. Yes. Very well, in fact."

Neither mentioned the elephant in the room.

Needing to do something with her hands, she added more double-sided tape to the corners of the banner in the large window. He probably felt as if he had to say something to fill the void, and opted for "I heard you interviewed Bert Bartholomew."

She did that thing with her nose again. "He knew his liquor," she said. "I'll say that for him."

"But?"

Ruby felt him looking at her, and she swore he was thinking it was good to see her. It didn't matter that the rubber band was slipping from the ponytail at her nape or that her nail polish was chipped and there was a big tear in her T-shirt.

He. Genuinely. Truly. Liked. Her.

And vice versa.

She was in trouble. Deep trouble.

"I didn't hire him, though," she said.

"Bert worked for us for a while at the orchard. He kept a flask in his chest pocket." Moving Joey to his other shoulder, he said, "I suppose bartending would be a better fit for him than running the cider press. What time was the interview?"

"Nine this morning." She pulled a face. "I own a bar. Obviously I don't have a problem with people enjoying alcohol."

"Just not for breakfast?" he said.

He was being very agreeable. She thought he looked tired and uneasy, which wasn't like him.

Just then someone with a soft, decidedly Southern voice called through the open door. "Reedykins, are you in there?"

Reedykins? Ruby thought, as a petite woman wearing white jeans, a pink shell trimmed in faux leopard skin and four-inch heels joined them inside.

She stood close to Reed and glanced around. Spying Ruby, she said, "I do declare it's taken us half an hour to walk down the street. Reedykins knows everyone in town and everyone is just so friendly."

Ruby caught Reed cringing.

Reaching a delicate hand toward Ruby, the curvaceous blonde said, "I'm Cookie Nelson."

Reed cleared his throat and after a barely perceptible pause, completed the introductions. Naturally predisposed to like nearly everyone, Ruby had no intention of liking Cookie Nelson. It seemed to her that failing to tell Reed he had a child, and then deserting her baby with no explanation, was a good enough reason to hold a grudge against her. While Ruby was silently justifying her position, Cookie looked up at Reed. And smiled.

And Ruby was pretty sure it was as genuine as the

stars in her eyes. "My mama always said it's the curse of small towns, don't y'all agree?"

If Ruby could have found her voice she might have agreed, but it didn't matter. Cookie carried the conversation by herself. In almost no time Ruby learned that blue eyes ran in Cookie's dearly departed father's side of the family and her grandmother had loved apple pie, which apparently was some sort of a sign from heaven, since Reed lived on an apple orchard.

For an elephant in the room, she was very petite and friendly and quite pretty. Perhaps a year or two older than Ruby, she wore pink well, and that Southern drawl was almost contagious. She may have been a little ditzy and she may have talked a mile a minute about nothing, but she called Bell's Tavern "an adorable drinkery."

No matter what she'd done, Cookie Nelson wasn't going to be an easy person to dislike.

And Ruby wanted to dislike her.

"Y'all are opening on Friday? This Friday?"

Ruby's gaze swung from Reed to Cookie and back again. He wouldn't bring her, would he? "Yes," she finally said.

With a bat of her eyelashes, she gazed at Reed, and said, "We haven't been out yet. Do you think we could attend?"

"I don't think—"

Before he could finish, Cookie turned to Ruby and said, "We have a lot to work out, as you can imagine."

Joey let out a little squawk. The sound the baby made seemed to remind Reed where he was, what he was doing and that he had to go. His gaze found Ruby's. Sensing his reluctance, she swore he wanted to say something. The moment passed, and the trio left, Cookie taking two steps to Reed's every one and Joey riding contentedly in his favorite position at Reed's shoulder. Watching them go, Ruby thought it would be so much easier if the blonde bozo were easier to hate. It would be easier if Cookie were, too.

Was she Joey's mother or wasn't she?

Why was she in Orchard Hill if she wasn't? And why hadn't the private investigator moved on to his next case? It was all Ruby could do to keep from grinding her teeth together in complete frustration.

Casting a surreptitious glance over her shoulder at Ruby, Cookie daintily tucked her hand into the crook of Reed's arm. It was a possessive gesture if Ruby had ever seen one. Cookie Nelson wasn't stupid, not in the least.

And she wasn't going to be so difficult to dislike.

On Friday, Reed read through the contract on his desk. The terminology was important, the details even more so, and yet when he reached the bottom of the page, he didn't remember a single word he'd read. This was one time an eidetic memory would have come in handy.

The faraway drone of Marsh's chain saw carried on the warm breeze wafting through the open window. He'd gone out a few hours ago to clean up fallen tree limbs in the orchard. Noah and Lacey had returned from their honeymoon and were now in Traverse City visiting Madeline.

On Joey patrol this morning, Reed listened intently to the baby monitor on his desk. He was reassured by the baby's soft breathing and the occasional hum he made in his sleep, but distracted by the sound of narrow heels clicking across the hardwood floors.

Cookie's footsteps didn't stop until she reached the doorway of Reed's office. She wore jeans and a flowered top, the neckline low and the waist cinched tight. There was a provocative pout on her lips. "I made you a glass of iced tea," she said in her soft Southern drawl.

Reed put the contract down and flattened his hands on top of it. Sashaying closer, she perched daintily on the corner of his desk.

"It's iced tea, Southern style. Although I must say I can think of something a lot more fun to do while Joey's sleeping and we have the house to ourselves."

Reed ignored the overture and took a perfunctory sip of the icy beverage. It was syrupy sweet. Like her.

"It's an acquired taste, Reedykins. Maybe if you'd give it a chance."

She was pretty. She was provocative. She was even sweet. Perhaps she was right, and sweetness was an acquired taste.

But she wasn't telling the truth about Joey.

She had to realize that Reed, Marsh, Noah and Sam doubted her story, for they hadn't left her alone with Joey since she'd arrived. She'd been tearful that first morning. Crying daintily into a pack of lavender-scented tissues, she'd told them how sorry she was for leaving Joey that way and how afraid she'd been and how alone. Finding herself all alone, without family and few friends, she'd had the baby blues, she said. Reed had asked his family doctor about postpartum depression. It was a serious condition, so they'd all treaded lightly.

"Give me a chance, Reedykins?" she whispered

from her position on the corner of his desk. Reaching down, she laid her small hand on his arm, the action leaving him a clear view of cleavage.

Reed met her gaze instead, and held it until she looked away.

He could have learned to drink sweetened tea and to live with pink everything, with shoes in every room and gossip magazines on the coffee table. The Reedykins handle wasn't easy to swallow, but he supposed he could have learned to live with that, too. He might have been able to forgive her for abandoning Joey and for failing to so much as tell Reed she'd been pregnant. Perhaps in time he would have been able to forget.

But something was off with her story. And he didn't believe it had anything to do with postpartum depression. Sam was working on the case and they were all waiting for the results of the paternity test to arrive. Meanwhile, Cookie was evasive.

And seductive.

"It's the redhead, isn't it?" she asked.

Reed was saved from answering by Joey's cry. Cookie glanced at the monitor and slid to her feet.

"I'll get him," Reed said in no uncertain terms.

Her eyes narrowed, but she stepped aside and let him pass. Reed made a beeline for Joey's nursery. "Hey, buddy," he said from the side of the crib. "No wonder you're mad. You rolled over again. You don't like tummy time, remember?"

He picked the baby up, and instantly Joey quieted. Reed's heart swelled. His chest, too.

He'd watched Cookie closely with Joey. She was gentle with him, but until she produced proof that he was her child, Reed and his brothers weren't about to lower their guard where the baby was concerned. And she'd produced no proof.

She claimed she'd lost Joey's birth certificate when she'd been evicted from her apartment shortly after his birth. Sam had assured her, all of them, that that wasn't a problem. She could simply contact the county where Joey had been born and obtain another copy. As far as Reed knew, she hadn't even tried. Her memories of her pregnancy and Joey's birth were vague and inconsistent. Whenever Reed, Marsh, Sam or Noah asked pointed questions, her face crumpled and the weeping began anew.

Reed wasn't buying the act.

Laying Joey on the changing table, he was certain Cookie knew it. He unfastened the tabs on Joey's diaper. The instant the diaper was off, the baby kicked his feet in wild abandon. He'd first displayed the new little quirk two days ago. Already, he'd changed so much. He'd changed them all.

"I know," Reed said softly. "You love being naked. We're going to have a little talk about that when you're older."

Joey's gaze locked with Reed's and his grin widened beguilingly. He grasped two of Reed's fingers in his small, perfect hand. It made fastening the tabs on the new diaper more challenging, but Reed finished the task, disposed of the wet diaper and dressed him again.

Picking Joey up as if he'd been doing it all his life, he turned, and found Cookie watching him. She stood in the doorway, her blue eyes misty and her voice quavery. "It really is the redhead, isn't it?"

"Do you know what I think, Cookie?" he asked, starting toward her, Joey in his arms.

"What, sugarplum?"

"I think we should keep this about you."

A memory from Reed's childhood washed over him just then. His great-grandfather had been a well witcher. It sounded like voodoo, but in reality it was simple science, not magic. Holding a thin metal rod in each gnarled old hand, his grandfather had walked across a plot of land, north to south, east to west. When the divining rods crossed, he stopped. And invariably there beneath the ground the well-digging company found water.

Once, Reed asked how the rods knew. His grandfather had explained that water produced a different frequency, a different energy than dirt, rock and soil. And those divining rods sensed it the way an honest man sensed the truth.

There was a bit of his great-grandfather's wisdom in Reed as he studied Cookie's expression today. "Why are you here?" he asked.

She didn't cry into a lavender-scented tissue this time.

Wearing a pretty flowered shirt and a sad wistful smile, she gazed back at him, as dainty as a Texas bluebonnet. And just as hardy.

If Reed had been holding his great-grandfather's divining rods, they would have crossed. That was how close he was to the truth.

Chapter Twelve

"Is he here yet?"

Oh, boy, Ruby thought. Not this again. It had been a lot easier to pull off blasé when the he in question had been Peter. The atmosphere at Bell's Tavern was charged with anticipation. She'd been watching the door all night, and she wasn't the only one.

Rumor had it Reed was coming.

From her position behind the bar, she performed a quick scan of the room. The hardwood floors and the ornately carved bar were gleaming. The lights were turned low and nearly every table was full.

The live music was loud and the dance floor was crowded. Reed wasn't on it, though. He wasn't sitting at the bar or playing pool in the back. He didn't throw his cards on the table and yell, "Misdeal."

It was too early to call the grand reopening a complete success, but the waitstaff had barely had time to come up for air.

"Is he here yet?" Abby Fitzpatrick stood on tiptoe trying to see over so many tall people.

Ruby looked from Abby to Chelsea, and caught the dark-haired wedding planner averting her gaze. "What aren't you telling me?" Ruby demanded.

Chelsea studied her fingernails and coyly refrained from answering. Ruby knew nuances. Chelsea didn't want to lie.

Orchard Hill had an active grapevine, but this wasn't simply the rumor mill at work. Chelsea, Abby, Sam, Reed's brother Noah, Lacey and everyone else whose eyes were trained on the door expected something to happen.

Ruby understood how gossip traveled. Several people had seen her talking to Reed at Murphy's that night. Evidently someone had seen his car parked at the bottom of her stairs, too, and someone else had noticed him helping her carry boxes from her car into her tavern.

Reed and his brothers had grown up in this town. The Sullivans' past was tragic, their personalities alluring and their smiles tempting. In case that wasn't enough to cause hearts to flutter, someone had left an innocent baby on their doorstep. Nearly a month later, a dainty and very stacked Texan arrived claiming to be the baby's mother. Who could resist talking about that?

Ruby, that was who. She filled four glasses with beer on tap and lined them up on a tray. She was mixing her first Kerfuffle when the bartender she'd hired returned from a short break.

"Is he here yet?" Natasha asked as she donned her apron.

One of the waitresses rushed to the bar, saving Ruby from replying. "I need a Dynamite, a Howl at the Moon and two Fountains of Youth." She pointed her finger at Sam Lafferty but smiled at Ruby and said, "So is he? Here yet, I mean."

One by one, Ruby eyed the people she knew best in Orchard Hill. No matter what Chelsea, Abby, Sam and Natasha claimed, they knew something Ruby didn't know.

Bell's new bartender had straight black hair and striking green eyes and was taller than Ruby. With her straight black hair and striking green eyes, she was beautiful. At six-one, her height put her at a definite advantage. She had a clear view of the door. Ruby saw her eyes widen. A moment later, Ruby's widened, too.

Someone new had arrived. Someone wearing tight white jeans and a pink tank and five-inch heels. Oh, no. It was Cookie. Ruby felt the strangest compulsion to run. But there was no place to hide.

The noise level rose and a gasp sounded. That might have been Ruby. From her position at the end of the bar, she saw Cookie scan the room. The instant she spotted Ruby, she started toward her.

She was halfway through the crowd when another gasp carried through the room. All eyes turned to the door again. This time it was Reed who'd entered.

He scanned the room, too. And while the band began to play another song, his gaze landed lightly on Ruby.

Noah cut in front of Reed. He must have told his brother Cookie was here, because Reed's entire demeanor changed. Ruby watched as Reed caught up with the little Texan with the big hair.

Funny, Ruby hadn't been jealous of the bottle redhead in Cheater Peter's bed. She'd been shocked, disgusted, insulted, scorned, hurt, humiliated and about a hundred other unpleasant things, but not jealous. But then, she'd only *thought* she was in love with Peter.

Maybe this wasn't love, either. Maybe it was lust. Perhaps it was the condition that occurred to people who survived terrifying events like bank robberies or getting stranded on desert islands. What was it called? Stockholm syndrome. Wait, it wasn't that. That was when a person fell in love with her captor, and that took years to overcome. Hopefully it wouldn't take Ruby that long to get over Reed.

Bother.

Ruby had known for weeks that Reed was looking for the mother of his child. She'd known he was a family man at heart, but seeing Cookie and him together was harder than she'd thought it would be. It made her chest ache, and her stomach, too. And that made her mad. *Ha.* It seemed it wasn't going to take her forever to get over him, after all. In fact, she was thinking about clobbering him over the head with the bottle of whiskey Natasha was opening. Ruby wouldn't, of course. She'd paid good money for that Jack Daniel's.

While she was still weighing the pros and cons of violence and vengeance, a strong arm came around Ruby's shoulders. "Hello, gorgeous," Sam Lafferty said. "I haven't gotten up close and personal with a redhead yet tonight. If you know what I mean."

"No need to get poetic," she said sardonically. "You had me at hello."

With that, the notorious P.I. and famed carouser led her into a two-step around the perimeter of the dance floor. Ruby knew what Sam was doing, but he couldn't block Reed and Cookie from her view entirely.

They were talking now. Reed looked angry. Before Ruby got close enough to see Cookie's expression, Jake Nichols, the local veterinarian, cut in and spun her in the opposite direction.

Digger Brown cut in next, followed by someone named Josh and finally that guy Ruby had talked to at Murphy's the other night.

Her head was spinning by the time a man cut in for the final time. This one was tall and smelled of a woodsy aftershave and night breezes and apples, of all things. His eyes looked gray tonight, his hand at the small of her back possessive.

"Reed Sullivan," she said sternly. "What do you think you're doing?"

Chapter Thirteen

The first thing a woman learned in dance class was to let the man lead. After all, the true test of a dancer's finesse was to follow, regardless of her partner's ability.

But Reed wasn't dancing.

Music was playing, and other people were shuffling backward and forward, to and fro. Reed had assumed a dancer's position, his fingers twined with hers, one hand on the small of her back. But he was standing perfectly still, his eyes on hers.

She'd worn black tonight, and pinned her hair in a loose knot on the back of her head. As far as Ruby could tell, Reed hadn't noticed her outfit or her hair. Since he'd cut in on that last dance, he hadn't taken his gaze off hers.

"You have to move your feet to two-step," she grumbled.

She'd spoken, and in doing so, she'd moved her lips, which apparently drew his gaze to her mouth. Before she reacted to his nearness, to his heat and the strength in his arms, she said, "Where's Cookie?"

Tightening his hold, not loosening it, he said, "With any luck she's in the cab I called for her, on her way to the airport to use her one-way ticket to Dallas."

The Madonna Mamas were playing a song by Faith Hill. They sounded so much like the original it was uncanny. Strangely, Ruby could wrap her mind around that. But she didn't trust herself to analyze what Reed had said.

"Where's Joey?" she finally managed to say.

"He's home. With his father."

Her eyes widened, her mouth opened and her heart pounded. "You mean. Cookie isn't— You're not— Joey isn't—"

Reed shook his head.

He started to move, drawing her into the dance. But Ruby wasn't having it. "Joey—he's Marsh's?" she stammered, her feet planted firmly on the floor.

This time Reed nodded.

"Oh, Reed. I'm so sorry. So, so sorry."

"No, you're not."

She did a double take.

"At least I hope you're not," he added. "I'm not sorry."

She heard the depth of emotion in his voice. "I wanted him. I still do. I'd take him in a heartbeat if Marsh needed me to. I'm disappointed. Deeply. But I've had all week to come to terms with it."

"What are you talking about?" she asked. "You've known all week?"

"I didn't have any proof, but I was pretty sure the first night," he said.

The music was so loud Ruby missed whatever Reed said next. Abby must have stepped in, because the next thing Ruby knew, the band was taking five and Abby was rubbing her hands together at a job well done. No one was dancing this dance, anyway. Everyone, it seemed, was watching Ruby and Reed.

He lowered his hand from the dancing position to his side, but he continued to hold hers, his fingers warm, his thumb moving in a semicircle over her wrist. "I helped Cookie into a taxi an hour ago. She was supposed to go directly to the airport."

"Why didn't she?" Ruby asked, and that was only one of the questions blazing through her head.

"Because her ploy didn't work and because she's a drama queen, and maybe to take a year off my life."

"That I can see," Ruby said. "But then why did she finally leave?"

As if he hated to admit it, Reed said, "Because she's not entirely evil. She wanted to tell you something. You see, Cookie really is alone in the world. Like a lot of people, she struggles to get by."

Ruby was watching him closely, listening closely.

A waitress brought Ruby and Reed something to drink and Sam shooed another couple out of their chairs so they could sit down. While activity resumed all around them, while a card game was lost and a billiards game won, while the Madonna Mamas began to play again, and Natasha served up whiskey and pale ale, Reed told Ruby that when a friend of Cookie's relayed that a P.I. had come to the restaurant where they used to work and was asking questions about a waitress named Cookie who'd apparently left a baby on a doorstep in a college town in Michigan, Cookie remembered Reed.

"She and her friend did a little research online, and they found my family's orchard and they thought maybe there was an opportunity here. She swears she never meant to hurt anybody. It was just a little white lie."

"Claiming to be Joey's mother was just a little white lie?" Ruby asked.

"Her words not mine," Reed insisted. "She only intended to keep up the facade until I fell in love with her, or Joey's mother returned, whichever came first."

He took her drink from her hand, set it on the table and reached for her hand in his. "I couldn't possibly fall in love with her. I love you, Ruby. I love your Florence Nightingale tendencies and your mile-long legs. I love your wild hair and your eidetic memory and how unafraid you are to try new things. I love that you love everyone. And I'm hoping you love me."

Just then, the Madonna Mamas began to play "YMCA." People flocked to the dance floor. Ruby and Reed didn't join in.

"Remember when you asked me what my favorite color is?" he asked.

Although she nodded, she couldn't help wondering what that had to do with anything. "Not pink," he said.

Ruby felt it, that quiet little mewling inside, a shared smile and that delicious uncurling of rose petals.

"What's wrong?" he asked.

"Nothing. Everything. I was just thinking we still have two hours before last call. And now those two hours are never going to end."

"Who says we have to stay until closing?"

They got up together, and skirted tables and the edge of the dance floor and the bar. While the Madonna Mamas crooned the iconic song, Ruby and Reed sneaked out of Bell's.

Maybe sneaking wasn't the correct term. The two of them were hard to miss, her red hair and swaying hips, his masculine swagger and shirt so white it practically glowed in the dark. He turned Ruby into his arms before the door closed behind them, and covered her mouth with his. Already breathless, they started up the stairs hand in hand.

"Is there something you'd care to tell me?" he asked at the top.

"I can't think of anything," she said.

She knew what he was waiting for. She was waiting for the perfect time.

He swung her into his arms like a groom carrying his bride over the threshold. Ruby gave a little yelp, because it looked a lot easier in the movies. Maureen O'Hara's shin never banged against the doorjamb and Humphrey Bogart's hip never smashed into the doorknob hard enough to leave a mark.

But this wasn't the movies. This was real life. And in real life, Ruby laughed out loud and they both groaned a little in pain. Their gazes met, and their breathing deepened, and he loosened his hold and let her slide slowly down his body.

"Which way to your bedroom?" he asked.

She led the way. There, she switched on an old metal fan and a lamp with a fringed shade. He opened a window, she turned down the bed and finally they stood facing each other.

He laced his fingers with hers, palm to palm, and slowly went down on one knee. "There still isn't anything you'd care to say to me?" he asked.

"There is one thing," she said. "As long as you're down there, would you do me a favor?" He quirked one eyebrow. Oh, he had a dirty mind. One more thing to like about him.

"I dropped an earring earlier. I think it went under the bed. But never mind. Come here, would you? I'd like you to be standing for this."

He rose and stood feet apart, hands on his hips.

"You were saying?" she asked.

"Do you know when I knew I wanted to marry you?"

Her breath caught. "Actually, this is the first I've heard you want to marry me, but go ahead. I'm listening."

"It was the night I watched you eat a quart of ice cream by yourself."

It was the last thing she'd expected him to say. "You fell in love with me because I went overboard eating ice cream?"

"I fell in love with you because you don't do anything halfway."

"I thought you were going to say you knew last weekend when I was wearing that white dress."

He shrugged, and it was a marvelous shifting of shoulders and man. "That's when I knew I had to have you in my bed."

"Oh," she said. "Well, that's pretty, uh, I was going to say straightforward, but it occurs to me that I like a straightforward man."

He took both her hands in both of his and held them,

just held them. The fan whirred, and just like that, the lamp on the dresser went out.

"I think that's a sign," she said. "Did I tell you I'm superstitious?"

"The first time I saw you, you asked me what sign I was. You said I was a water sign, deep and moody."

"I really am sorry about Joey, Reed. I know how much you love him. Although I must say it is nice to know you're good with babies. I'd like to have a baby, your baby, maybe a few, maybe twins, a boy and a girl."

"Would you marry me first?" he asked.

"I'd want Father Murphy to perform the ceremony."

He inched a little closer, nudged her hair from her temple with his lips. "You want your old boyfriend to marry us?"

"That's what I like about you." Her voice was growing husky, dusky. "You always understand."

"That's what you *like* about me?" He was still waiting to hear her say it.

"There are a lot of things I like about you. You're a snappy dresser, for one. And underneath that cool, calm and collected persona is a streak of very uncivilized man."

He was feathering kisses along the side of her face, her cheekbone, below her ear and just beneath the ridge of her jaw. She pressed her body against his and kissed him, once, twice. His breath was a rasp as she tugged his shirt from the waistband of his jeans and undid every button. He was a patient man, but when she slid her hands underneath, pressing the fabric up and off him, he shuddered and took over.

"Do you know when I knew I loved you?" she asked as he whisked her silky black shirt over her head.

He caught her raised hands in his, and clasped her wrists together in his right hand. She felt shackled, and she swore she'd never felt such a delicious shudder go through her.

"This is the first I've heard anything about love," he said, his voice husky, his hips pressing against hers.

He was going to make her say it. She liked that about him, too.

"I knew I loved you when I heard you ask Nanny McPhee if she'd ever been spanked." He laughed, and even though she was serious, she didn't mind, because sometimes serious life was pretty funny.

"I've loved you every moment since, even when I hated you, even when I wanted to clobber you over the head with a perfectly good bottle of whiskey."

He lifted his face and looked at her, his eyes dilated in the semidarkness. "That sounds like true love to me. Is there anything else you want me to know right now, Ruby?"

"I can't think of anything off the top of my head," she said.

He placed her hands on his shoulders and whispered, "You're going to want to hold on for this."

She tipped her head back and smiled. But she did hold on, and on, and on, through kisses, and sighs, and murmurs and a serenade as old as time. Their remaining clothes came off slowly, shoes, slacks, her skirt and a pair of fine cotton panties.

He eased her onto her back on the bed, the fan whirring, the mattress shifting beneath their weight. He covered her breasts with his hands and covered her body with his. She was tall. He was taller. She was soft and unbelievably pliant, and he was hard and un-deniably strong.

She was underneath him one minute, sprawled on top of him the next. She giggled when he found a tick-lish spot, and he let all his breath out when she wrapped her legs around his hips.

He had her on her back so fast she gasped. She opened her mouth beneath his, and he began to move. The mattress shifted and the curtain fluttered at the window, their only music. She made a sound deep in her throat, until the shudders overtook her, and him.

Sometime later, he eased to his side and drew the sheet to their shoulders. Her long curly hair tickled his chin, and his short blond chest hair tickled her nose. They smiled in the near darkness, and it was as if the whole universe smiled with them.

"So this is love," he said.

"Who knew?" she agreed.

Not Reed, until he met Ruby, and not Ruby, until she met Reed.

Someone opened the door downstairs, and voices called to one another from the alley. Bell's grand re-opening had been a huge success. Ruby was already looking forward to her next adventure. But no matter what she tried next, she was putting down roots here in this town where Johnny Appleseed once visited, where Reed's great-grandfather once discovered water, and his mother, rain. She was putting down roots with a man who knew how to make an entrance, and would always want to make an entrance with her.

They would never agree on ice cream and neither would want to cook, but he would read to her, some-times from the newspaper, other times from one of the books stacked on his nightstand. She would love everyone in his family, even his great-uncle, the judge. And he would love her mother, and respect her father and tolerate her uncle Herb.

Later, she would tell him that someone had made her an offer to buy Bell's tonight. But for now, they touched, they enticed, they enjoyed, they aroused. They promised to be true and faithful, to love each other forever. She felt like a bride already, and it was better than in the movies. She made love to the man she loved, the man who loved her in return.

Her. And nobody else.

And him, and only him.

* * * * *

*Don't miss these other stories in
Sandra Steffen's* ROUND-THE-CLOCK BRIDES
series:

*THE WEDDING GIFT
A BRIDE UNTIL MIDNIGHT
A BRIDE BEFORE DAWN*

Now available from Harlequin Special Edition.

COMING NEXT MONTH FROM

HARLEQUIN®

SPECIAL EDITION

Available June 24, 2014

#2347 FROM MAVERICK TO DADDY
Montana Mavericks: 20 Years in the Saddle! • by Teresa Southwick
Rust Creek Falls newcomer Mallory Franklin is focused on providing a stable home for her adopted niece—*not* finding the man of her dreams. But Mallory just can't help running into ravishing rancher Caleb Dalton everywhere she goes! Still, she's got to stand firm. After all, carefree Caleb isn't exactly daddy material...or is he?

#2348 A WIFE FOR ONE YEAR
Those Engaging Garretts! • by Brenda Harlen
When Daniel Garrett and Kenna Scott swap "I do"s in Las Vegas, the old friends know the deal. This marriage is just to help Daniel access his trust fund, and it will be dissolved before they even know it. But, as the hunk and the blonde beauty find out, their marriage of convenience might just turn into a lifelong love—and a forever family.

#2349 ONE TALL, DUSTY COWBOY
Men of the West • by Stella Bagwell
Nurse Lilly Lockett is on a mission—to heal the patriarch of the Calhoun ranching clan. Then she meets the irresistibly rakish Rafe Calhoun, the ranch's foreman. Love has burned Lilly in the past, but the remedy for her heartbreak might just lie in the freewheeling bachelor she's tried so hard to resist!

#2350 SMALL-TOWN CINDERELLA
The Pirelli Brothers • by Stacy Connelly
Debbie Mattson always put family first—until now. The beautiful baker has finally reached a point in her life where she can enjoy herself. But there's a roadblock in the way—a big, *hunky* one in the form of her lifelong friend Drew Pirelli. Drew's got it bad for Debbie, but can he help her build her happily-ever-after?

#2351 A KISS ON CRIMSON RANCH
by Michelle Major
Sara Wellens has *had* it with Hollywood! The former child star is dead broke, until she finds out she inherited part of her late grandmother's Colorado ranch. There, Sara butts heads with former bull rider Josh Travers, who wants to make the ranch a home for himself and his daughter. Has the single cowboy met his match in a former wild child?

#2352 THE BILLIONAIRE'S NANNY
by Melissa McClone
Billionaire AJ Cole needs to ward off his family's prying, so he produces an insta-girlfriend—his assistant, Emma Markwell. The brunette charmer agrees to play along, but fantasy turns to reality as the two share passionate kisses. When AJ claims he just wants a fling, Emma resists. Can she show the tycoon that she's all he needs—now and forever?

———————————

YOU CAN FIND MORE INFORMATION ON UPCOMING HARLEQUIN® TITLES, FREE EXCERPTS AND MORE AT WWW.HARLEQUIN.COM.

HSECNM0714

REQUEST YOUR FREE BOOKS!
2 FREE NOVELS PLUS 2 FREE GIFTS!

H HARLEQUIN®

SPECIAL EDITION

Life, Love & Family

YES! Please send me 2 FREE Harlequin® Special Edition novels and my 2 FREE gifts (gifts are worth about $10). After receiving them, if I don't wish to receive any more books, I can return the shipping statement marked "cancel." If I don't cancel, I will receive 6 brand-new novels every month and be billed just $4.74 per book in the U.S. or $5.24 per book in Canada. That's a savings of at least 14% off the cover price! It's quite a bargain! Shipping and handling is just 50¢ per book in the U.S. and 75¢ per book in Canada.* I understand that accepting the 2 free books and gifts places me under no obligation to buy anything. I can always return a shipment and cancel at any time. Even if I never buy another book, the two free books and gifts are mine to keep forever.

235/335 HDN F45Y

Name _____ (PLEASE PRINT) _____

Address _____ Apt. #

City _____ State/Prov. _____ Zip/Postal Code

Signature (if under 18, a parent or guardian must sign)

Mail to the Harlequin® Reader Service:
IN U.S.A.: P.O. Box 1867, Buffalo, NY 14240-1867
IN CANADA: P.O. Box 609, Fort Erie, Ontario L2A 5X3

Want to try two free books from another line?
Call 1-800-873-8635 or visit www.ReaderService.com.

* Terms and prices subject to change without notice. Prices do not include applicable taxes. Sales tax applicable in N.Y. Canadian residents will be charged applicable taxes. Offer not valid in Quebec. This offer is limited to one order per household. Not valid for current subscribers to Harlequin Special Edition books. All orders subject to credit approval. Credit or debit balances in a customer's account(s) may be offset by any other outstanding balance owed by or to the customer. Please allow 4 to 6 weeks for delivery. Offer available while quantities last.

Your Privacy—The Harlequin® Reader Service is committed to protecting your privacy. Our Privacy Policy is available online at www.ReaderService.com or upon request from the Harlequin Reader Service.

We make a portion of our mailing list available to reputable third parties that offer products we believe may interest you. If you prefer that we not exchange your name with third parties, or if you wish to clarify or modify your communication preferences, please visit us at www.ReaderService.com/consumerchoice or write to us at Harlequin Reader Service Preference Service, P.O. Box 9062, Buffalo, NY 14269. Include your complete name and address.

Looking to create his own legacy, Daniel Garrett wanted out of the family business. But the only way to gain access to his trust fund was to get married. So he convinced his best friend, Kenna Scott, to play the role of blushing bride. What could go wrong when they sealed their "vows" with a kiss that set off sparks?

***

"You set out the terms," she reminded him. "A one-year marriage on paper only."

"What if I want to renegotiate?" he asked.

Kenna shook her head. "Not going to happen."

"You know I can't resist a challenge."

Her gaze dropped to the towel slung around his waist and her breath hitched.

She moistened her lips with the tip of her tongue, drawing his attention to the tempting curve of her mouth. And he was tempted.

One simple kiss had blown the boundaries of his relationship with Kenna to smithereens and he didn't know how to reestablish them. Or even if he wanted to.

"Aren't you the least bit curious about how it might be between us?"

"No," she said, though her inability to meet his gaze made him suspect it was a lie. "I'd prefer to maintain my unique status as one of only a handful of women in Charisma who haven't slept with you."

"I haven't slept with half as many women as you think," he told her. "And I know what you're doing."

"What?"

"Deflecting. Trying to annoy me so that I stop wondering what you're wearing under that dress."

She shook her head, but the hint of a smile tugged at the corners of her mouth. "There's French toast and bacon in the oven, if you want it."

"I want to know if you really wear that stuff."

"No, I just buy it to take up storage space and torture your imagination."

"You're a cruel woman, Mrs. Garrett."

She tossed a saucy smile over her shoulder. "Have a good day, Mr. Garrett."

When Kenna left, he poured himself a mug of coffee and sat down with the hot breakfast she'd left for him.

He had a feeling the coming year was going to be the longest twelve months of his life.

***

Don't miss
A WIFE FOR ONE YEAR *by award-winning author*
Brenda Harlen, the next book in her new
Harlequin® Special Edition miniseries
THOSE ENGAGING GARRETTS!
On sale August 2014,
wherever Harlequin books are sold.

Copyright © 2014 by Brenda Harlen

HSEEXP0714

HARLEQUIN®

SPECIAL EDITION

Life, Love and Family

Coming in August 2014

ONE TALL, DUSTY COWBOY
by *USA TODAY* bestselling author
Stella Bagwell

Nurse Lilly Lockett is on a mission—to heal the patriarch of the Calhoun ranching clan. There, she meets the irresistibly rakish Rafe Calhoun, the ranch's foreman. Love has burned Lilly in the past, but the remedy for her heartbreak might just lie in the freewheeling bachelor she's tried so hard to resist!

Don't miss the latest edition of the *Men of the West* miniseries!

Look for THE BABY TRUTH, already available from the
MEN OF THE WEST *miniseries by Stella Bagwell!*

Available wherever books and ebooks are sold!

HSE65831

HARLEQUIN®

SPECIAL EDITION

Life, Love and Family

SMALL-TOWN CINDERELLA

Don't miss the latest in
THE PIRELLI BROTHERS miniseries
by **Stacy Connelly**

Debbie Mattson always put family first—until now.
The beautiful baker has finally reached a point in
her life where she can enjoy herself. But there's a
roadblock in the way—a big, *hunky* one in the form
of her lifelong friend Drew Pirelli. Drew's got it bad
for Debbie, but can he help her build her
happily-ever-after?

Available August 2014
wherever books and ebooks are sold!

www.Harlequin.com

HSE65832

Love the Harlequin book you just read?

Your opinion matters.

Review this book on your favorite book site, review site, blog or your own social media properties and share your opinion with other readers!

Be sure to connect with us at:
Harlequin.com/Newsletters
Facebook.com/HarlequinBooks
Twitter.com/HarlequinBooks

HREVIEWS

HARLEQUIN®

A *Romance* FOR EVERY MOOD™

Stay up-to-date on all your
romance-reading news with the
Harlequin Shopping Guide,
featuring bestselling authors, exciting new
miniseries, books to watch and more!

The newest issue will be delivered right to you
with our compliments! There are 4 each year.

Signing up is easy.

EMAIL

ShoppingGuide@Harlequin.ca

WRITE TO US

HARLEQUIN BOOKS
Attention: Customer Service Department
P.O. Box 9057, Buffalo, NY 14269-9057

OR PHONE

1-800-873-8635 in the United States
1-888-343-9777 in Canada

Please allow 4-6 weeks for delivery of the first issue by mail.

HSGSIGNUP